— Phoebe Lauren —

GAREV PUBLISHING INTERNATIONAL

North American Address

5840 Corporate Way, Suite 200
West Palm Beach, FL 33407
Tel: (561) 697-1447   Fax: (561) 477-4961

European Address

50 Highpoint, Heath Road
Weybridge, Surrey KT13 8TP
Tel: (44) (0) 1932 844526   Fax: (44) (0) 1932 820419

©Phoebe Lauren
©2004 Garev Publishing International

ISBN: 0 9707558 2 1

All rights reserved. No part of this publication may be reproduced, stored in a retrieval system or transmitted in any form or by any means, electronic, mechanical, photocopying, recording or otherwise, without the prior permission of the copyright holder.

STAR CHILDREN
Among us

DEDICATION

Star children, I dedicate this book to you and the success of your mission. It's impossible to list all of your names, but you know who you are.

I am deeply grateful to my former husband, Jim, who over the years has offered so much support. And, of course, I want to thank my parents for telling me at age twelve that I could be anything I wanted to be and for all the love shared with my mother over these past years since I struck out on my own to be a writer.

Finally, I want to express my gratitude to Gene Evans and Marta Garrido of Garev Publishing International who have made this book a reality in the English language.

Phoebe Lauren

Savitri

I saw the Omnipotent's flaming pioneers
Over the heavenly verge which turns towards life
Come crowding down the amber stairs of birth;
Forerunners of a divine multitude,
Out of the paths of the morning star they came
Into the little room of mortal life.
I saw them cross the twilight of an age,
The sun-eyed children of a marvellous dawn . . .
Discoverers of beauty's sunlit ways
And swimmers of Love's laughing fiery floods
And dancers within rapture's golden doors,
Their tread one day shall change the suffering Earth
And justify the light on Nature's face.
Although Fate lingers in the high Beyond
And the work seems vain on which our heart's force was spent,
All shall be done for which our pain was borne.

Sri Aurobindo

STAR CHILDREN
Among us

Part 1

Chapter One:

Who Are the Star Children?

All human beings are created equal. Who believes that? How many Mozarts are there versus those who can play the piano? Who can hold a brush in their hand and produce a Monet? Yet, while we are all born with a variety of talents and capacities, we all have something in common. We humans are able to reflect on our lives and actions. There is something inside of us, call it a soul if you will, that seems to exist independently of our bodies. And this is the part, if I dare to say so, that is "created" or "shared" equally by all.

We are all born into a "clan", whether we like to admit it or not. All of us were born somewhere, in some location on Earth. As babies we may have heard wild animal calls, or the sound of someone delivering milk over cobble-stoned roads, or the sirens and street noises of a big city. Most of us were born into a religious practice, the spirit of a nation, a certain race of people. In other words, there are always circumstances surrounding a birth, much like a setting on a stage when the curtain opens on the first act of a play.

And what happens after we are "on stage"? We each have the capacities and gifts necessary to "play our roles". Some of us become "stars" and have big roles to play and others are in "supporting roles". Some of us have strong bodies and play football; others are frail and stay home to write poetry. We come in all physical shapes and sizes, not only as individuals but also as nations.

We also come with different intellectual abilities. No one would argue this – one visit to a scientific facility or to a home for those who are learning challenged is sufficient proof. Have you ever known someone who could learn a foreign language in a few months while you struggle for years? Or the person who can play any tune after hearing it once and you can't remember a thing after ten years of lessons? No two of us are alike, just as every flower and leaf in nature is different. There is infinite variety on Earth and subtleties beyond our understanding. So within the human species there are those things that we all have in common and then the myriad of individual differences.

Just as some of us identify with a certain race, religion or group of people, there are those of us, myself included, who have an affinity for the concept of being a Star child. Star children exist in every nation, in every race, at every age level. They have come to Earth from distant stars to aid Planet Earth and its inhabitants – to bring peace, hope, and joy to troubled hearts and warring nations.

Star children have certain characteristics, exactly as there are people with musical talent, artistic talent, and other capacities. Almost all Star children share the collective belief and remembrance that they have come to Earth from another star, vibration or planet. Since I have heard many differing descriptions of this "place of origin", it is not clear to me if the star is an actual place in the universe, a vibration, or a dimensional reality. This remembrance may be present at birth or may come gradually over the years. Also Star children have a deep soul longing to return to their star and have difficulty understanding the human situation – especially cruelty and competition.

Star children have come to Earth as peacemakers and see that as their primary mission. Many choose to work in the helping or healing professions, which include environmental ecology to heal the Earth. It seems that the awareness of the existence of the spiritual world is heightened and that there is a recognition of oneness with the Spiritual Source, or Essence. Perhaps this is needed in order for Star children to fulfill their Earthly mission. While the mission is a collective one, there is a full representation of the human family, each person having an individual role to play.

How do Star Children fit in with the other groups of "new children"?

There are reports of identifiable groups of the "new children" incarnating on the Earth at this time. Some of you may have heard of them. Although my research is limited, as is all research, I have read most everything available about these "new children" on the Internet, in books and articles. It seems that many people, especially therapists and educators, became interested in these "new children" when suddenly so many children were not able to learn under the traditional teaching methods. More and more children are showing clear signs of "learning differently" and in order to aid these identified children, interest was peaked.

So far, in addition to the Star children, I have found the following groups identified:
1. The term *new children* is being used in Holland
2. There are *the super psychic children* who are clustered mainly in China
3. Some children are developing or being born with *super immunity* which some say is a direct result of the AIDS virus
4. There are the *Indigo children* whom many think are the system busters.

Before you read any further, let me say that I have not verified the existence of some of the above groups of children, nor do I personally know the people who have identified them. This information is offered for comparison purposes only and if you have further interest, you must pursue these reports yourself. Some of them may be fictitious, others may contain statistics misconstrued, and some may be wishful thinking. Since my work is focused only on the Star child phenomenon, I do not believe it is for me to verify other people's theories; but in order to give you, the reader, the most comprehensive picture possible, it seemed that reporting upon these groups was a necessity. The information and facts, which support my ideas, come from personal experiences, years of study and research, interviews and comments of Star children, plus information, which has been received during my meditation sessions.

I believe that before we are born, we decide or it is decided for us, what particular gifts and challenges we will have at birth. Whether our personality and body type is decided by our heritage or by our soul consciousness or a myriad of other possibilities is not especially interesting to me. The fact is that we all arrive with certain talents, certain abilities that can be put to use in order to express ourselves and to contribute to the society into which we are born. For instance, someone who is born in an isolated mountain village in Nepal probably doesn't need to learn to speak three to four languages to have a productive life, but the child born in Holland does. And the Swedish child's body isn't equipped as well as the African child's body to withstand the heat and sun of the desert.

We are all part of the human community. Each one of us is an important expression of the Divine. Yet the Star children have particular attributes and challenges. If you're a Star child, you may be having visions which you don't understand, be frightened by knowing the future, be able to see your loved ones after they die, or be too sensitive to operate as a "normal" human being. Who's to say it's normal to eat hamburgers, go to discos, watch violent movies, kill each other, or even read the newspaper?

I think it's fabulous that people are beginning to speak up and identify all these different groups of children. Let's have all the theories and propositions we can about how to help our children, ourselves and other Star adults everywhere. Let's not all try to be the same. Let's make each child special and unique. Let's appreciate the gifts that all children bring.

Personal Experience:

New Children – Holland

The only organization for new children that I have had personal contact with is in Holland. I've had the opportunity to participate in events held by the *Platform for New Children* (Platform Nieuwe Kinderen) and to present my ideas about Star children. The Platform provides a venue for a wide range of therapists, educators and parents to put forth their ideas, theories and approaches in dealing with children. It serves as a referral agency and sponsors events and presentations about children, often including young people themselves. The Platform does not identify with any one definition of the "new children" nor does it endorse any special approach or therapy, as far as I can tell.

Research:

Super Psychic Children

Let us now look at the different groups of children that have been identified through my research. According to an interview on 'Children of the New Dream' with Drunvalo

Melchizedek, a New Age author and lecturer who has some very interesting theories, the first super psychic child was discovered in 1984 in China. When the child's psychic abilities were tested, he was right one hundred percent of the time. The people from *Omni* magazine, a U.S. publication, assumed this was a hoax, so they conducted their own tests. "They did experiments like putting a hundred kids in a room and taking a book and randomly pulling out a page. They would crumple up the page and stick it under their arm. These kids could read every word on the page. They did test after test, and the response was flawless"[1]. Since then, these super psychic children have been found in other parts of the world.

Children with Super Immunity

In the same interview, Drunvelo pointed out that identifying the children with super immunity started at UCLA hospital, a major university hospital in Southern California. A young baby tested positive to the HIV virus at birth and at one-year-old. He converted to negative status sometime between one year and six years of age when he was tested again (by the way, it is not abnormal for a baby to test positive to the virus at birth if his mother is carrying the virus, and then to convert to negative sometime during the first year of life). At UCLA, this child's DNA was tested. In the human DNA we have four nucleic acids that combine in sets of three, producing sixty-four different patterns that are called codons. Human DNA all over the world always has twenty of these codons turned on, except for this boy who had twenty-four codons turned on – four more than any other human being. The scientists found, by conducting experiments with his blood, that the child was immune to every known disease. At this point, according to UCLA statistics gathered from watching worldwide DNA testing, there is approximately one percent of the world population or sixty million people who have this new DNA.

Drunvalo believes that this new DNA is accessible to anyone because it is now in the subconscious of the Earth – much like a morphogenetic field. A morphogenetic field is composed of "complex structures (which) may arise from the interaction between units that have characteristics such that they can fit together in a certain way"[2]. So, to use more understandable language, a morphogenetic field is an overall energy field into which we as human beings can enter and fit. For instance, if everyone around you can speak several languages, theoretically, it will be easier for you to learn different languages. If you go to Holland where practically everyone can easily ride a bike, you can enter into that morphogenetic field of "bike riding" and more easily ride one yourself. At least, this is the theory!

Drunvalo believes that others can access this super immune state through deep meditation and prayer in three parts. He explains exactly how we might do this. The first part is that the mind must see the unity in all – that nothing is separate. The second part is being centered in the heart – to be loving. And the third part is to stop judging so that we no longer are in the polarity of good or bad, right or wrong. He believes "these people (with the new DNA) have somehow stepped out of judging and are in a state where they see everything as one and feeling Love"[3].

Indigo Children

The fourth identified category is the *Indigo children* described in a book of the same name. An Indigo child is "one who displays a new and unusual set of psychological attributes and shows a pattern of behavior generally undocumented before. This pattern has common unique factors that suggest that those who interact with them (parents, in particular) change their treatment and upbringing of them in order to achieve balance. To ignore these new patterns is to potentially create imbalance and frustration in the mind of this precious new life"[4].

The first person to identify this group was Nancy Ann Tappe in her book, *Understanding Your Life through Color*. Nancy has worked in the field of parapsychology for twenty-five years and worked closely with a university in southern California in conducting experiments that verified her intuitive findings. Somewhere in the seventies, she noticed the Indigo children, which is the color she "sees" as their life color. She looks at people's life colors to learn what "their mission is here on the Earth plane and what they're here to learn." In the eighties, she started to label this phenomenon of the Indigo children.

Nancy says that these children are computerized and that they are more in their heads than in their hearts – children born for the technological age. While Nancy says some pretty unusual things about Indigos, her four different categories into which she divides these children may serve a purpose. (She claims that all children who kill other children are Indigo and goes on to state that ninety percent of all children under ten years old are Indigo!)

The categories are:
- *Humanist* – who will serve humanity, are hyperactive, extremely extroverted and easily distracted, who will be the future doctors, lawyers, teachers, business people
- *Conceptual* – more into projects than people, very athletic, have control issues, especially with their parents, and tend toward drug addictions, who will be engineers, designers, astronauts, military officers
- *Artist* – sensitive, creative, and like to experiment with many different creative arts, tomorrow's teachers and artists
- *Interdimensional* - larger in physical size than the other Indigos, very sure of their knowledge, self directed, come from other planets, and will bring in new philosophies and religions[5].

Of course, many other groups of children have been written about including the intuitive child, the sensitive child, the psychic child, and the creative child. The distinguishing factor in the above categories is that we are now identifying groups or clusters of new children who seem to have more or less the same attributes.

Star children may be part of any of the above categories, as they usually have psychic abilities, may have super immunity (if there is such a phenomenon), and some have probably come on the Indigo ray and/or are part of the interdimensional category of Indigo children. I have personally "seen" Star children with the following life ray colors: pink, red, green, purple, blue, and indigo. However, I'm not completely clear if what I "see" is exactly what is being referred to in the Indigo theory of life colors.

Star children then are just one of the numerous new categories of physical beings who are incarnating at this time. Although there have always been Star children on Earth, this current large wave of incarnations has been going on for about fifty years. It is being noticed now for the first time as the wave peaks, more about this in Chapter Four.

Chapter Two:

Are You a Star Child?

Many people ask how they can tell if they are a Star child or if their children are. I am a Star Child and have had the privilege of having a son who was one. In fact my interest in Star children began with his ideas and beliefs. I have written the account of his amazing life, death, and reincarnation in a book entitled *Star Child*. Since that time I have been focused on this phenomenon. I have met, befriended, and counseled Star children in Europe, Mexico, Canada and in the U.S. According to my direct experience, here are some characteristics, which most Star children seem to have (of course not every Star child has every one of them).

Characteristics of Star Children

Deep spiritual awareness

There is a profound connection with spiritual aspects of life, often accompanied by communication with Angels, guides, a "loving voice", or even God. This deep connection with the aspect of love energy makes it very difficult to understand the current human situation on Earth. The moon, the stars, and the sun often obsess Star children, who spend hours stargazing. They love the light – all things that glitter – gold – brilliance. There seems to be a process of transformation, of having an open connection to the light, to the All, to the Source. This awareness also means that Star children know that everyone is connected to one another and if someone disconnects emotionally or physically, they feel the pain right away.

They perceive that not everyone remembers the Source – they come as teachers. One Star Child, age seven, shares: "We are all part of God and life polishes us until we attain perfection"[6]. A three-year-old, named Jackie, told her parents that "God is in everything – I can see it"[7]. And of course there's that wonderful story that many of us have heard about the little boy who asked his parents repeatedly if he could talk to his newborn sister alone. Finally, the parents said it was okay, though they thought it was a strange request. The little boy walked over to his sister's crib and asked, "Will you please tell me about God? I am starting to forget."

Remembrance of other realms

For Star children, there is a remembrance and a longing to be somewhere else, where people and things work together with greater harmony, peace, and love. Earth energy seems hard and "foreign". There is little understanding of the human states of competition and greed. This is coupled with the belief that everyone on the Earth should cooperate. They don't understand why there has to be separation – different nations, languages, and religions – if these things cause less joining with the whole. There is an awareness that what happens to one person happens to everyone. If one part of creation is injured, for instance, the Earth, everything and everyone suffers. Star children come as spiritual teachers – to bring the knowledge and love which they "remember" to the Earth plane.

Flavio, a Star Child, at age eight wrote: "Babies cry because to live on this planet is very difficult. A baby tries to express himself with his telepathic voice, but it doesn't function here because everything is too dense... The newborn is terrorized by his imprisonment in the physical reality"[8].

Robert, at age four, was very excited to have a new computer, though he was a little disappointed. He said to his mother, "It sure isn't like the one I used to use. I guess they don't make them as fast or good as they used to". Another Star child, named Mark, age fifteen, had made a series of drawings of UFOs, as well as "various technical schematics of the propulsion systems that drove each one, which he understood and could describe in detail. He is considered by his teachers to have a graduate school level understanding of physics"[9].

Feelings of not belonging

There is a feeling of being left out, of not belonging on the Earth, of not being accepted, of being different. Candice, in her mid-twenties, shares this feeling with us: "From the beginning I knew that something was different about me, although I didn't know what. I remember my first day of kindergarten so clearly, walking into the group that was already situated around our teacher. I walked into the group and immediately knew that something was very strange and that I really didn't belong there. The other kids, from day one, literally began to treat me as though I was an alien or something"[10].

I had a similar experience when first going to school. I fully expected to be at a "wisdom school" where I would learn about why I was here on Earth and how things worked. There are a few lucky Star children who have had such experiences where they actually attended hidden "wisdom schools" on Earth. Many Star children seem to be coached in special schools at night. Dr. Richard Boylan reports, "Scores of experiencers have told me about going at night to a special location on Earth, or up into a spaceship, to be shown and taught many things, including events of the near future. These Star kids may not understand everything they have been shown at the time, but later, when it will be important, the information comes or will come to the surface of their mind to be used"[11].

Another author, Caryl Dennis has reports of children "going to school at night with their friends and acquiring very advanced knowledge, to which their parents know they could not have been exposed in everyday reality. Where and just what this school is remains a mystery, although one often hears that it is on a ship of some kind, indicating again the possible involvement with the children of some non-human intelligence. Until our understanding of the true nature of this mysterious universe we inhabit is considerably deeper, we can only speculate on the nature of such phenomena"[12].

One Star child, who obviously attended another type of school at one time, reported what normal Earth school was like, "You know at school here, when the teacher says something's going to be hard, it's easy, and when she says it's going to be easy, it's hard. I guess they learn differently on the planet I come from"[13].

The feelings of not belonging diminish when one Star child meets other Star children. Once there is actual contact with others in the Star family the feelings of being different disappear and are replaced by a deep understanding and newly found awareness. Flavio, age six, upon meeting Aïda, a transpersonal psychologist, breathed a sigh of relief: "Finally, I have met someone like me! She has the same mission as me. I feel really alone on Earth. Now, I know that we are numerous and that our mission is to tell the things that we know even though everyone knows and feels them. . . Human beings will begin to be different; children are going to be more open to the spiritual"[14].

I cannot begin to tell you how important it is to connect with others of like energy. Many, many people who come to me for sessions are put at ease in their lives just by meeting me – because they no longer feel alone and isolated on Planet Earth.

High level of balance

There is usually high level of functioning of all attributes normally associated with the left hemisphere of the brain: rationality, intellect, and analysis and those of the right hemisphere: intuition, imagination, creativity and synthesis. These children are being born with the ability to use their whole brain, depending on the circumstances. That is to say they can think globally or concretely – they can use their intuition on the material plane.

Star children tend to be very quick for their age, reading and talking at an unusually early age. There are reports of babies speaking when they are just a few weeks old, and many use vocabulary and concepts well beyond their chronological age. These children seem at home with complex equipment and have the ability to operate computers without the least bit of fear, contrary to what is experienced by many of their parents. In other words, Star children seem to be born with an understanding of how to use the equipment they will need to communicate their message of peace to the world. They have been described as "adults in children's bodies" and as "old heads on young bodies".

Many Star children end up combining two or more careers that reflect this balance and high level of functioning. Since I could never choose what career to have, a dilemma that many Star children share, I decided to be everything I wanted to be. So I'm an English teacher, an attorney, an artist, an author, an interfaith minister, a workshop leader and lecturer, and the list will go on for as long as I'm here. In fact, it's quite common for Star children to combine divergent careers and practice them at the same time, for instance, the scientist/sculptor; the translator/flutist; the medical doctor/artist. Don't get caught into thinking you must choose one or the other. This can cause an unnecessary problem and delay. I tell Star children that any career is possible – no matter how old they are!

Because of these abilities, Star children will change systems, especially the educational one; but they are not "system busters" (as some define Indigo Children), nor are they likely to be diagnosed as having one of the attention disorders. If you should be the parent to such a child, you will know it! Then I encourage you to read the book, *Indigo Children*, which was mentioned earlier. Please do this before you accept drugging your children as a method of behavior modification.

Star children will change the systems by using their exceptional abilities with love, in a peaceful way. They are learning to understand and experience the physical world in which they have incarnated, while remaining in contact with the spiritual world – their star or origin.

Hypersensitivity

Star children often have acute sense of hearing, taste, touch, sight, and smell. When they are young, they may report that certain lights or loud sounds actually "hurt" them and that some smells literally make them "sick". They may be able to see beyond the visible light spectrum, which enables them to see things that human beings ordinarily cannot. One mother reported that her daughter could see colors around everything and that sometimes the sky seemed to be purple. Another child is not able to eat with metal utensils because he can taste the metal when his tongue touches it. Some children are so sensitive that their clothing bothers them; the labels in their clothes are painful. Others can wear only natural fabrics and then the soap they are washed in must be carefully chosen. Many Star children cannot tolerate fluorescent lighting and feel disoriented in shopping malls, large stores, and schools. Some children can smell odors like cigarette smoke a block away. It is interesting to note that these sensitivities can vary from day to day as well. One day a food may taste too bitter to eat and the next day it is just fine.

Because of this hypersensitivity, Star children often cannot tolerate and will often overreact to medicine. Even a simple aspirin may bring on a bizarre reaction. Some suffer from allergies to things that no one else is apparently allergic. These children heal faster and easier with alternative healing methods, such as homeopathy, Bach Flower Remedies, nutritional modifications, and color and sound therapy. I believe that Star children are just more sensitive to everything in general and that this can be looked upon as one of their challenges and as one of their gifts. Often this sensitivity in early years of life will lead them into careers having to do with healing through alternative therapies or ecological pursuits, thus enabling them to fulfill their Earth mission.

Some Star children report that they are simply too sensitive to stay on Earth and they want to leave, and in fact, some of them do. If you find yourself dealing with a child who is having trouble living on Earth, it is essential that you seek out alternative medicine practitioners because often nothing can be diagnosed with normal medical tests. You child is not "making things up" – you just have to find a person who knows how to work in a different way. Star children can be easily taught how to cope with and improve their state of sensitivity.

Psychic abilities

Many Star children have psychic abilities, which come as a part of being multidimensional. Star children come from the higher dimensions and enter the limited dimensional awareness of life on Planet Earth in order to help in its evolution towards a new dimension and higher vibration. So it stands to reason that in order to fulfill this mission it is of necessity to "remember" how to see and do things differently. These children are more intuitive than average and often have imaginary friends who are very real and exist in other dimensions. There is a great love of nature and an ability to connect with plants, minerals and animals – as if there is no difference in life forms.

My own son, Marcus, who was a Star Child, had spiritual guides around him who had helped him prepare for his lifetime before he was born and who guided him through his lifetime on Earth. He often spoke to them and called upon them for advice. Marcus could read auras at an early age and had many spontaneous past life recalls. He was able to foretell the future, even his death, which was "his return to the green planet" where his "mother" still lived[15]. He also predicted the exact circumstances of his future incarnation and told me that I would know him again in his new life, and this has come to pass.

For a number of years now, I have served as a spiritual counselor along with my other work of giving workshops and lectures about positive thinking and the book, *Star Child*.
I remember counseling one little boy who was about seven-years-old. He had seen "Angels" around his mother who told him that she was going to die. His mother had cancer. He

wanted to know if it would be all right to tell his mother that the angels would take care of him and that she could give up her fight to live. He also was aware of his guide who had been with him since birth and knew that he'd be just fine, although he was going to miss his mother.

Another young person reported to me that she couldn't tolerate walking down the streets or going to school because the "colors" of the other people always went into hers. She couldn't understand why others didn't also see these colors, which form a vibrational energy field around each person and is called an "aura". I've also seen many, many drawings by children where they've colored auras around people and even one little girl who made auras around plants and animals. She was convinced that even "doggies" have colors!

Some day there will be schools where Star children can learn and have the freedom to use their psychic abilities and talents. Here they will be able to explore their limits (or lack thereof) and to interact with other Star children. I can imagine these schools will be a bit like the one which our famous fictional little friend, Harry Potter, attended to learn about magic[16]. The children will all be having fun, knowing that they are surrounded by others like themselves – with teachers who understand – who are "different" themselves. What a day of great joy that will be!

Dr. Richard Boylan is already planning schools for Star children where they can "learn and have freedom to use the advanced abilities and talents they have ... without the ridicule or negative peer pressure they would face in ordinary schools. Such schools will also have a component for parents, where these mothers and fathers will get guidance on how to help their Star Kids truly be all that they can be. And there will be help for their parents to come to terms with their own journey from ordinary "reality" to the cosmic society into which we are rapidly evolving"[17].

Natural sense of justice

Star children have a natural sense of justice, of right and wrong, which is stronger than in most human beings. By justice, I don't mean in the judicial sense, but in a spiritual sense. Star children naturally believe that it is wrong to kill, to harm anyone or anything. For instance, these feelings and beliefs may lead many to become vegetarians in a family that is not strictly vegetarian.

In recent years, I had the great honor of attending a festival for the "new children" as they are called in Holland. At one point, there was a very beautiful blessing over a huge crystal bowl of water. Then little glasses of "energized" water were given out. It was amazing how many small children, between the ages of three and five took a little plastic glass and handed it to their siblings, friends, or parents, before they took a glass for themselves.

There is a natural sense of sharing, as if the concept of "mine" and "yours" is a bit foreign. A Star child explains, " A new child knows that he or she is part of All. If one tries to teach him the idea of "mine" or "for me", she or he doesn't understand. She or he is not able to dissociate "mine" from the All and thus believes that all belongs to everyone. He or she must be allowed to share. There is only one "Me" for "All", although the individual "Me" has infinite variety"[18].

Old souls; Many lives

Star children often recall their past lives, especially when they are quite young. I've heard of children speaking to their birth parents about their parents that they had before, in a past lifetime; and even one little girl who told her mother that she, the mother, was her daughter in a life before. My son, Marcus, remembered his previous three short lives and that he had experienced different ways of dying in order to gain information about Earth life. He also believed that his real "mother" was at home on the green planet from which he came. Because of this, he refused to call me mother and eventually settled on and gave me the name "Phoebe".

Past life recall is quite common in children everywhere, regardless of the beliefs of their parents, up to the age of seven when the Earth plane vibrations begin to be solidly in place. This is the same moment that many children stop speaking about "imaginary" play mates and they no longer see or hear the spirits in nature. Star children frequently remain connected and don't lose these abilities.

To me, it had always made perfect sense that Star children have had both previous lives on Earth plus lives in other realms. I was quite surprised to be able to verify this idea. When I give lectures, I often ask the question and have found that many adults believe their soul originated on another planet or star and yet they've had previous incarnations on Earth as well.

There are some people who believe that Star children have come to Earth from higher dimensions and that it is their first time on Planet Earth. Well, I believe that anything is possible and that there is no need to have great discussions about this. In any event, everyone who is doing research on these children agree on one thing – they are different – their consciousness is higher or more expansive than the norm and they are here to help human beings evolve to a higher awareness of love and light.

Other people's ideas about Star children

On one website I discovered a very sincere and well thought out presentation about "Star people" by a "Star Person". There, a list of qualities of Star people was presented and it is one of the best I've found in all my research. This list, which is reproduced here, gives a real sense of who we are:[19]

- Loneliness, as if you do not belong here or do not have family here
- Impatient with Earth life, used to doing things instantaneously (do you ever accidentally walk through furniture as you move to the other side of a room?)
- Very sensitive, to the point of having a hard time "blending" . . dislike of killing animals, of hurting others, etc.
- A late bloomer
- Empathic (picking up others feelings and thinking they are your feelings)
- Dislike of crudeness or harsh behavior
- Talents in areas such as understanding advanced physics, healing or working with crystals, thinking in symbols and colors rather than words, telepathic, clairvoyant, healing abilities, etc. Talents can run a huge range of expressions, but they will be out of the norm, and the use and expression of them is expanding to whatever field you are in. It may be that you are a counselor and your ideas expand people's sense of what is possible. You may pioneer a new branch of study in some field. You may light up a room just by walking into it.
- You are in a rush, as if you are on a mission, and you have limited time.
- A sense that you really don't belong here. . . no sense of home, or roots.

Here's another questionnaire that is not meant to be used as a self-questionnaire, but one you may wish to use to determine if someone close to you is a Star child[20]. Although Ms. Randles' book presents the idea of an alien conspiracy, which is a highly controversial subject, there is some valuable information in it. Remember with all printed material, we must be discriminating – even when you are reading what I'm writing. As I said before, I am attempting to give a comprehensive picture of the Star children phenomenon and feel compelled to present different viewpoints.

The questionnaire

1. Do you have any unusual phobias, such as fears of certain colors or a reaction to a particular word?
2. When out driving or walking is there an area that you will make a long detour to avoid, even if you are not conscious of why you are doing so?
3. Have you seen what you are pretty certain was a UFO on more than one occasion – if so, how often?
4. Have you had a number of vivid dreams about aliens and UFOs?
5. Do you dream normally in color and recall at least two or three dreams every night? Have you had flying, floating or lucid dreams?
6. When you read the words Sobec-alp do they create any unusual feelings? What kind of feelings?
7. Did you develop a sudden intense interest in the following: space, ecology, antiquity, psychic phenomena, the sea, mysticism or fountains?
8. At what age did you have the earliest vivid memory that you can check for accuracy with other family members?
9. As a child did you ever experience, or talk to your family about, strange figures or odd light effects appearing in your bedroom?
10. Between the ages of three and ten did you ever believe that your wardrobe could move or even talk to you?

11. Do you have an interest in, or enjoy attempting, poetry, creative writing, chess, logic puzzles or art?
12. Have you ever had periods in your life when more than half an hour of time – or some awareness of space and distance – has disappeared and you cannot remember how or why?

While I don't understand some of the questions, for instance the sixth one, it did seem apropos to include the questionnaire here. More than anything, I believe that the above questions can trigger a memory which may be deeply buried and which could point you in the direction of your origins.

And on another site, I discovered a list of attributes of "Star people", compiled by Brad Steiger who has written many books on this subject. He links current day Star people to Native American beliefs in the creation of human beings by visitors from the stars. Following is an abbreviated list of attributes, which includes those experienced by seventy percent or more of Star people[21].

- Their eyes have an extremely compelling quality
- They have great magnetism and personal charisma
- They are very sensitive to electricity and electromagnetic fields
- 88-92% have lower body temperature than the norm
- At an early age they had some kind of extraterrestrial, religious or mystical experience
- 92% feel a tremendous sense of urgency to fulfill their missions
- 65% are female; 35% are male
- 90% have experienced a sense of oneness with the universe
- 83-94% have chronic sinusitis
- 97% have hypersensitivity to sound, light and odors
- 93% have pain in the back of the neck
- 84% adversely affected by high humidity

- 71% have difficulty dealing with/or expressing emotions
- 74% report out of body experiences
- 75% have experienced clairvoyance, clairaudience
- 72% claim an illumination experience
- 90% have experienced telepathic communication with another entity, physical or non-physical from another realm
- 76% believe in reincarnation and have past life memories
- 78% believe they have lived on another planet and can tell you about it
- Some are aware of parallel existence at this time in other worlds
- 86% believe in miracles
- Most believe in a God or creator energy source
- All believe in life on other planets

Common traits of Indigo Children:

I think most people who are interested in "new children" would agree that the book *Indigo Children* is about the most comprehensive one written to this point. It is a collection of reports and comments by accredited children's workers, teachers, Ph.D.'s, M.D.'s, and authors all over the U.S. Unfortunately, comments from other countries were not included, so the book has a distinctive "American flair."

The Indigo Child is defined as one who "displays a new and unusual set of psychological attributes and shows a pattern of behavior generally undocumented before." Here are ten of the most common traits of these children:

1. They come into the world with a feeling of royalty (and often act like it).
2. They have a feeling of "deserving to be here," and are surprised when others don't share that.
3. Self-worth is not a big issue. They often tell the parents "who they are."
4. They have difficulty with absolute authority (authority without explanation or choice).
5. They simply will not do certain things; for example, waiting in line is difficult for them.

6. They get frustrated with systems that are ritual-oriented and don't require creative thought.
7. They often see better ways of doing things, both at home and in school, which makes them seem like "system busters" (nonconforming to any system).
8. They seem antisocial unless they are with their own kind. If there are no others of like consciousness around them, they often turn inward, feeling like no other human understands them. School is often extremely difficult for them socially.
9. They will not respond to "guilt' discipline ("Wait till your father gets home and finds out what you did").
10. They are not shy in letting you know what they need.

It's important that you have this information as you read on so that you can draw your own conclusions. Are Star children and Indigo children part of the same group? Are Star children a subgroup of Indigos? In my opinion, while both groups share many of the same characteristics, they are two different groups, though some Star children may also be Indigo children, and vice versa. The major difference that I see is that Star children are love beings who know that we are all One and are here to teach that in a peaceful way.

Chapter Three:

Why Are Star Children on Earth?

Star children incarnate in clusters at times of spiritual transition, and most of us will agree that now is a time of great change. They are here to help usher in the Golden Age of Spirituality in the New Millenium. Many of us are moving away from a world which is dominated by material things, external pleasures which are never long lasting, and are beginning to turn inward to gain real peace and true satisfaction. We are in fact becoming more spiritual.

All one has to do is take a look at the number of recent best selling books to see proof of this trend. Self-help books, channelled books and spiritual adventure books are now making the New York Times bestseller list. These are books that were once available only in "New Age" or metaphysical bookstores. Now, we can walk into almost any bookstore, grocery store, discount outlet, or international airport and find books with a spiritual focus. This is occurring also in European countries, Canada and Mexico. I don't know about the other countries; but surely with Internet, these books are being read far and wide. The media has caught on – spirituality is hot!

The history of the Star people goes back centuries. There are many well-known legends in Central and South America about *Star beings* coming down from the heavens to help humankind. One has merely to look at ancient drawings to see "extraterrestial" beings. Many of you are aware of the numerous theories about the pyramids in Egypt and in Central America being constructed by "extraterrestials".

Star people are playing a part in the traditions of the Indigenous Nations as well. In June 1996, the Native American Elders gathered at the Yankton Sioux Reservation in South Dakota for *the Star Knowledge Conference and Sun Dance*, which was convened by Lakota (Sioux) spiritual leader Standing Elk in response to a vision. The vision showed that it was the moment to share indigenous knowledge about the Star Nations.

The following information is taken from a report on the conference made by Dr. Richard Boylan. Standing Elk, Lakota Keeper of the Six-Pointed Star Nation Altar, said in his opening remarks that Medicine Men (and Medicine Women) have the ability to communicate with spiritual entities such as those of the Star Nations. The system of the Star Nations was based on mental, spiritual and universal laws. Oglala spiritual advisor Floyd Hand spoke about Avatars (world religious teachers) including White Buffalo Calf Woman who was the Star person that gave the Sioux their spiritual history, health practices and ceremonies. He said that the world's Avatars such as Jesus, Buddha, and Mohammed are Star people.

There is a long legendary history in the indigenous culture of Star people coming from the Pleiades, Sirius and Orion. There are also references to the blue and green Star people in the indigenous legends, and Standing Elk asserted that "the way of the stars is in every culture"[22].

At the *Star Knowledge Conference* in Sedona, Arizona in 1998, Hehaka Inazin (Standing Elk), a Ihanktowan Dakota declared that "it is time to start listening to the children who are born at this time; they carry messages." Clearly, something sacred is happening on Earth[23]. Children of today will be the ones to lead us into a totally transformed world, which the Native Americans call the Fifth World.

It is interesting to note that the six-pointed star is also known as the Star of David and that the Jews were forced to wear it on their clothing during World War II. The star itself is made up of two interlinking triangles – one that points up to the heavens (Father Sky) and one that reaches down into Mother Earth. The little Jewish children who were made to wear the yellow star during the Nazi occupation of World War II were known as the "Star children". So many little star souls who met such violent deaths must be shining down on us every night when we remember them and all those "stars" who died because of their religious beliefs, their national origin, their physical deformities, or their sexual preference during that dark time on Earth.

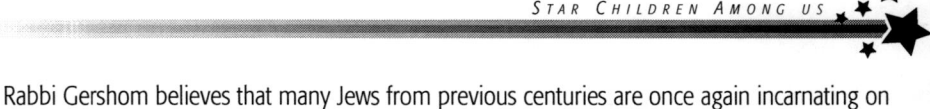

Rabbi Gershom believes that many Jews from previous centuries are once again incarnating on Earth, now that more than fifty years have passed since the Holocaust. He believes these souls are able to access the spiritual knowledge that they carry with them from pre-Holocaust incarnations. The Rabbi pointed out that the Native Americans believe in reincarnation and that they "attribute their recent cultural revival to the return of the souls of 'medicine people' who died a hundred years ago. These people, it seems, are 'remembering' the ceremonies that had been lost so long ago"[24]. Interesting to note that the six-pointed star is symbolic of both cultures! And that so many people are saying the same things in different ways. And why shouldn't Star children spread themselves across all cultures, all nations, and all religions?

It seems then that Star children/adults have always been with us on Earth. These are the sacred ones who bring higher spiritual knowledge down to the Earth plane. I believe it is only now that we are reaching a level of consciousness evolved enough to recognize a phenomenon that has been with us since the beginning of human kind. As a collective whole we are able to acknowledge that something different is appearing through our children because we are now able to "see" this new evolution of our race.

We adult Star children are becoming more comfortable in taking our place in the scheme of things. We are willing to risk being identified and at the same time being challenged. If you are a Star child, you are a natural peacemaker. Because of your higher vibration, arguments and lack of agreement cause you great distress and bring much sadness to your soul. Often times you prefer to walk away from disharmony, knowing that it is no use to try and make someone understand your point of view – before she or he is evolved enough to do so. Whether anyone acknowledges the presence of Star children or not, they are here. Some report that there are over one million Star children and adults already here. One has only to search the web to realize they exist.

So the soul path of a Star child is to be a peacemaker, to help Planet Earth evolve to a higher dimension as a Star of Love and Light. Star children have come from far, far away to help save Planet Earth and the people on it. They carry the message of unconditional love, unlimited hope, and much needed courage to all human beings.

Where do Star children come from?

Some of the Star children messengers come directly from another star or planet, while others are interdimensional beings, with the ability to go between dimensions. Star children seem to originate on a dimension of greater sensibility, of finer vibrations than that found on Earth. On these stars or vibration levels of origin, everyone gets along. Peace and harmony are ever present. Some say they come from the Pleiadides, others from distant green or blue stars. What is sure is that they come from dimensions undreamt of and unseen with human eyes. They are here, ready, and equipped to help in the peace making process.

When Flavio's mother asked him what was his star, he answered, "Each of us has a star. My star is all my energy in me. My star is golden"[25]. My son, Marcus, believed he was from the green star. Whether this was a real *star* or just a vibration, we will never know. This lack of precision should not take away from the overall concept.

In Holland, I met a young woman, a Star child, who was very concerned and sad after she read about Marcus' beliefs in my book. He believed that the red star was one of violence and evil. With tears in her eyes, she told me that she was sad that Marcus thought that the red star was evil because she was from there, and the beings were very kind and filled with love. What did I believe, she asked. I told her that there were millions and billions of stars in the universe and that I certainly believed that both she and Marcus could be right. They were just speaking about two separate stars, which were probably in different constellations. It is paramount that we don't make these children feel that their beliefs are strange or wrong. Open-minded acceptance with a strong sense of inner balance is essential when listening to these accounts and working with these children.

What is the exact mission of this current wave of Star children who are presently on Earth?

The mission of Star children is to work unceasingly to help with this transitional period on Earth, where human beings and the Earth itself is in the process of becoming less physical and more spiritual. They bring their gifts of wisdom, harmony and balance to Earth. Star children have chosen to come here as "Emissaries of Light", to show the way back to the Light or Source. One way that I attempt to bring more light vibrations to Earth is to stay connected with every person that I'm with, to the best of my ability. When someone says something positive or negative, I attempt to understand that it has everything to do with the person who is sharing and little, if anything, to do with me. In this way, I am able to stay peaceful no matter what is going on around me – and of course this strategy doesn't always work.

Star children are remembering or already know how to raise their vibrations to high levels. This is part of the transformation process in which the Star children will regain their original state. This "new state", which is natural, will aid in the realignment of human vibration. Whenever anyone is internally peaceful, there is more peace in the world; and we must find the peace present within, before we can speak of making a more peaceful world.

According to information, which I have received in deep meditative states, the stars of origination and the beings on them are more evolved than Planet Earth and its inhabitants. There, the inhabitants have already undergone the transformation in consciousness, which is now beginning to occur here.

Here is one Star Child's remembrance of her planet:

"The people of my home all look very much alike. They have big, beautiful, soulful, blue eyes that are slanted slightly. Their bodies are all white, with no mouths and no ears that I could see. They are extremely sensitive and communicate telepathically and with clairvoyance. They do not exist in the dense physical dimension we experience here. I noticed they do not seem to touch the ground when they walk. They do not need to eat food or do all the things to live that we do. However, I saw that there were many pine trees all over the place. The sky was darker than here on Earth, but very blue. I did not see any buildings or mode of transportation. The people appear to move by thought . . ."[26]

And here's a description of my son Marcus' star: "The people on my planet live under a glass dome, which keeps the air and pressure correct for us. My planet is very beautiful, but in a different way than Earth. We don't have trees, nature, oceans, or animals – only people. But I love it there because the energy is perfect. We are never tired or angry. We spend a lot of time sending good energy to each other.

"We don't miss anything because we can think up scenes and they appear before us. For example, I can go to the special room and sit and imagine a lake and then I will really be there at the lake fishing. This would seem like magic to you, but for us it is quite normal.

"It's a place where everyone gets along with each other... People there talk to each other just by thinking of the other person. Because we are happy and clear, we don't have to lie to each other or feel ashamed of something we do. So we have plenty of energy. We are all working on the healing ray, which is green. There's peace on our planet all the time".

I agreed that it sounded like a lovely place where we would all like to live and told him that while I didn't specifically remember such a place, I did have an ancient corresponding memory.

Chapter Four:

When Did Star Children Start Incarnating?

The following information was received in visions during my meditations. There is, of course, no way to "prove" any of what follows, except for you to go deep within yourself to verify and accept whatever part of it feels right. I offer it to you hoping that it will provide an opening in your thoughts and a broadening of acceptance of other ways of knowing.

Planet Earth and all life on it, including humans, were on a collision course. Mother Earth sent a call out into the Universe. It was a call of distress, a call for help from all higher vibrations. This call was sent out during World War II when the Earth and all life on it was on the verge of being totally destroyed due to the creation and use of the atomic bomb.

When the call was received in the vast Universe of Stars, those who had the capability to do so began to communicate with each other. That is, those stars and their inhabitants with the necessary level of awareness received the message of distress from Planet Earth, created a strategic plan of action and undertook it. Initially all inhabitants responded to the distress call of Planet Earth. This is not exceptional as inhabitants of the stars, and the stars themselves comprehend and fully understand that everything is connected in interlinking energy.

Soon, as the situation worsened, a Planetary Commission was formed and requests were sent out for volunteers to become part of the network. This network had a certain mission, which was quite simply to save Planet Earth and as many of its inhabitants as possible.

Those who chose to go immediately were very old, wise souls whose energy field could withstand the conflict and aftermath of the war. Many of these beings had been on Earth during the war and were killed in the concentration camps, in combat and in other inhumane tortures. At that time, they were already attempting to raise the level of consciousness. You see there have always been Star children or peacemakers on Earth.

The current phenomenon, however, is different, because Star children are incarnating in a great wave, which started in the early 1940's and will reach its peak around the end of this current decade in 2010. This means that many Star children have children or even grandchildren who are of like vibration. The ones who came in as part of the baby boom paved the way for those who came later. The finer energies within the network started to incarnate around 1970, though some were not sufficiently ready or able to continue into adulthood because the limitations were too great in the third dimension. Many of those chose to leave (or die) and to reincarnate again at a later date when the energy field was more tolerable.

Some years after 1970, a Star child writes, "The new children are being born. They are a different type of human being, although there is nothing to verify this. I am only one of them, one of the first. Humanity is in the process of changing. The connection with the spiritual world is more open. Now, all children are able to maintain their oneness with the spiritual source, with their essence"[27].

Helen Wambach, in her book, *Life before Life*, offers this explanation from her study in which she claims to have hypnotized seven hundred and fifty people. She found that more than eighty percent of her hypnotized subjects said that they chose to be born in the twentieth century because "it would be characterized by a new development of spiritual awareness, a coming together of people to transcend their individuality through the realization that they are linked on higher planes."

Some recalled being eager to be born and claimed they were here to assist in a new development in mankind's history. When asked why they were on Earth, they responded that they wanted to learn to relate to others and love unconditionally, without being demanding or possessive. Twenty-eight percent said they had a role in teaching mankind to understand his unity and to develop his higher consciousness[28].

Another researcher, Caryl Dennis, claims that almost everyone she interviewed in her study of "prodigies" felt as though they're here on a "mission" of some sort. "Prodigies", a term used in her book, are people who as small children had an experience of telepathic contact with an extraterrestrial entity. After this contact, which usually took place outdoors, prodigies felt that their heads had been filled with all knowledge. Some prodigies felt they "must help humankind develop spiritually or be of assistance during the coming Earth changes. Others felt they must develop the technological breakthroughs they had been given -- technology usually of an ecologically beneficial nature. Almost all felt they had been given vital information of some kind to share with the rest of us"[29].

What's it like for a Star child to come to Earth?

Flavio reports: "Before birth, I could see everything, from all angles. My vision had no limits, because I didn't have physical eyes. It was the first time that I was close to a planet so dense. (He's referring to Earth here.) I had to prepare myself by passing by other planets where I was able to train myself for this physical dimension. It was like learning to write in the air without a pencil. But this experience was to be very different, very unusual because I was going to have a material body. I had to bring with me some basic pieces of data in order to be able to be here: for instance the concepts of 'yes and no', 'time and space'. This world is one of opposites"[30].

So indeed, we have all been very brave to come to Earth and we must acknowledge each other for this feat. For no matter how long ago we were born, we all needed a certain sense of adventure, a high level of trust, and a commitment to do what we came to do. This is not to say, by any means that Star children come in without personal issues, karma patterns and everything else that every human being has at birth. All Star children have their struggles and challenges just like everyone else.

Chapter Five:

Where are Star Children Incarnating on Earth?

Many of those who were born during the World War II or just after it chose to incarnate in countries where they would not be harmed by the ravages of war (especially those who were killed in concentration camps). These Star children often chose to be born in the Americas to multi-ethnic, international families. Exposure to cultural richness is important because the ability to speak and understand more than one language is an essential tool for peacemaking. Those born during the war therefore chose "safe" countries, especially Canada, United States, Mexico, and Central America.

Remember that many of these children are super sensitive to vibrations. Therefore, it would be extremely difficult to be born into a war zone even after the war is over. The vibrations of violence rest on the Earth for years and perhaps are never completely forgotten. I believe that the Earth has a memory just like we do. An example of this is the first time I was in Holland, I can remember arriving in Rotterdam and "seeing" the city destroyed. This vision occurred in a fraction of a second. At that time, I didn't know that the city had been bombed during W.W.II.

It was only later that I realized the extent of the German bombing of such a lovely city. When I was shown pictures of the aftermath, it was exactly how I had viewed it in my mind's eye. Is it any wonder that Star children would probably not put that or many other European cities on the top of their list when choosing to reincarnate in the earlier years? And my experience is replayed on a daily basis by Star children in diverse parts of the globe.

It seems that after a number of years, the vibration of fear and violence lessens, thus clearing the way for Star children to reincarnate in places, such as Europe, which were devastated by the war. The Netherlands, where so many languages are learned, is once again a favored place. I believe the Dutch people of all Europeans are the most open to new ideas and spiritual matters. Could it be because of their long history of trade, the people in this small nation are known as world travelers? And, of course, Star children continue to be born to multi-ethnic and international families everywhere.

The familial environment of preference is one where there are multiple languages spoken in the home and where there is tolerance and love of the differences among races. Travel and direct experiences of other cultures are also very important. It should be very high on your priority list if you are a parent of a Star child to expose him to other languages and cultures, even if you are not multilingual. The child needs to see and experience other cultures directly as part of his peace mission.

Parental acceptance of the individual Star child's idiosyncrasies is mandatory, as the majority of these Star children simply do not fit into traditional school systems or other social structures. These children do their best in alternative school systems such as Montessori schools, Waldorf schools and other Indigo-type schools[31].

Generally speaking, these children choose culturally rich environments, often near or in big cities. They have a need for alternative forms of education, which cannot often be found in small villages. The people in large cities are frequently more open to a wider range of human expression than are the inhabitants of small villages. Isolation is not something generally sought out by Star children, though they have a deep love and concern for nature.

Many Star children report having a sneak preview of their parents and their environment before being born to a certain set of parents. What are they looking for exactly? It is difficult to say, though I would suspect that they certainly seek an environment where at least one parent is of the same or a similar vibration. Certainly, a parent who is open to psychic happenings or one who is psychic him or herself would also be high on the list. I believe they look for families where more than one language is spoken. In my birth family, for instance, there were three languages spoken regularly. Almost of all, I believe these children seek an experience of unconditional love and harmony within the birth family.

So, where will you find a Star child? Most anywhere. And how will you know them? Look for that old wise look in their young faces – eyes that have seen everything before. You'll know that "look" the minute you hold a Star baby in your arms. It is unmistakable. By the way, being a Star child is an inner conviction or feeling. There is no one who can decide that for you or your child.

Chapter Six:

Welcome, Little Star Child

More than once, I have been asked how prospective parents might set the stage to welcome a Star child. My first question to them, usually the mother, is why do you feel drawn to the idea. After some discussion, it almost always turns out that one or both parents feel they have come here from another star. They often remember their feelings of separation and loneliness and wish to help another like themselves.

Ideally, Star Children attempt to be born into a family where both parents are able to welcome and accept their differences and gifts. Star children are seeking, and coming to, "enlightened and proactive parents who take parenthood seriously and a step beyond the mainstream"[32]. However, due to the current relational configurations, this is often not possible. Thus sometimes one parent understands and is more easily able to accept the child than the other. And make no mistake; a Star child is a stress factor in any relationship, so let's get prepared.

One thing to keep in mind is that a Star child will often set his or her own agenda in life from a very early age. My son, for instance, decided when he no longer wanted a baby bottle by throwing it across the room. He also decided when it was time to stop wearing diapers and that was just the beginning of his decision-making. So a parent who wishes to have a Star child should be very loving and balanced. I really loved my son with all my heart, which apparently made up for the fact that I often felt out of balance. Also, having a Star child wife and son was not an easy situation for my former husband, who is now one of my best friends. And who knows, he may even be a Star child himself!

Here, however, we are addressing the optimum conditions for birthing a Star child. Also, I feel that as the wave of births of Star children peak, higher and more aware souls are incarnating, making preparation almost a requirement. To set the stage, the first step is for the parents to examine their own relationship with each other. Is it a stable one? Do you, as a partner, feel truly settled and committed to the other person? Do you think about leaving and/or getting a divorce? These are important questions because above all else, the Star child requires stability from at least one parent and preferably both. So working on and examining your own primary relationship is obligatory.

Once you feel your relationship is solid, I would suggest doing some inner work. The higher your own vibration, the better possibility you have to attract a Star child. Remember, Star children have a specific mission and a finer vibration than most people; thus, you must raise your own vibration to be compatible. It is a well-known fact that negative thoughts lower your physical strength and surely darken your energy field. Thus, if you want to be a "beacon of light" for a Star soul to find you, you will need to "lighten up"!

In my workshops, I often conduct a simple experiment usually with the strongest looking person. That person is asked to leave the room. I then tell the rest of the class to think of something very positive when I say, "Think thought X". And when I say, "Think thought Y", they are to think of something negative – a sad or angry situation. Then the strong person is asked to come back into the room. I ask the person to extend an arm out and to resist as much as possible as I try to push it down. Normally, I can't make the person's arm budge. Then I ask the class to think thought "Y" and down it goes. The person is surprised and we continue to try, alternating between thought "X" and thought "Y". With the positive thought, the person is strong and with the negative, weak.

The experiment is conducted not to impress the participants, but to show them the power of thought and its negative and positive influence over us. We have all had days where we have awakened in a bad mood for no apparent reason. Often it can be because we had a dream that we don't remember or because we have slept badly. Then our whole day is colored by our negativity and nothing seems to go our way. Over many years, we have all filled our "backpacks" with emotions, thoughts, and issues that weigh us down. And this situation increases our density and lowers our energy. Some of us, in fact, feel tired all the time.

So you can just imagine how important it is to clear out long held anger, sadness, and disappointments, which you have acquired over a lifetime. Sometimes, people come to me and tell me that they want to have a Star child, and I always say, "Well, let's get to work". For an average person, I would say that working with a therapist over a period of about six months should be sufficient to prepare the territory. After all, before one plants a crop, one must till the soil.

The tilling of the soil is hard work. You are required to look at feelings and memories that you don't generally look at. It is not easy, but it will pay off once that child is born. So being the best and highest that you can be is a great beginning for you and your prospective child. Not only that, your primary relationship and everyone you come in contact with benefits when you do inner work. But just as in planting a crop, once the soil is turned, nutriments must be added to it. We aren't trying to "plant" any old seed here, but one that will produce a Star child.

What are the nutriments? Having a spiritual practice is very important, whether you meditate, go to a traditional church, use affirmations, or spend time with positive thought. It is important to not only reduce your violent, competitive thoughts, but to ameliorate the situation to the positive side.

Another consideration is your physical health. It is wise to have a check up and take care of any physical problems, as well as getting your teeth fixed. Whatever health issues you have should be taken care of promptly. When a Star child is in embryo, he or she responds particularly strong to any kind of medical intervention, necessary or not. Regular exercise, eating a balanced diet and not burning the candle at both ends are all good positive steps. Oh, and if you haven't stopped smoking yet, isn't your prospective child a good reason to do so? Drinking alcohol should be minimal, though I don't think a glass of wine at dinner ever hurt anyone.

You are probably wondering if all these suggestions are necessary and worth it. You may even be a Star child and be thinking that surely your parents didn't do any of the above, and of course, in the majority of cases, you are correct. Yet the question is how can you best prepare for birthing a Star child – not what is the minimum you can get away with!

Having considered all the above and hopefully you've kept those medical and therapy appointments, what is the next step? The first step is tilling the soil and adding the nutriments; the second is to "plant the seed". Before you go off the pill, or stop whatever kind of birth control you are using and jump in bed, stop for a moment and feel within yourself if this is the right time for you to have a baby. So many times, people have children because everyone around them is telling them it's time, or their friends all have or are having children, or they have nothing else to do. You must quietly ask inside if this is the appropriate time for you both to have a child. Of course, it goes without saying that both partners must be in agreement to attempt to have a child.

Exercise for going within and asking about the timing to birth a Star child:

The following exercise is so simple that you may doubt that it will work. Believe me, it will. Sometimes the simplest exercises are the best. Please read the exercise all the way through before attempting to do it.

You will need the following: a candle (optional), matches, and a selection of peaceful music.

You do this exercise with your partner when you are both in a relaxed mood. You may want to begin by placing a candle in the room and lighting it together. Any color is fine. Some couples are drawn to use a white candle as a symbol of their pure intention. When you light the candle, you can ask for guidance and also state your intention. For instance, you both might say something like this: "We are doing this exercise to come more in touch with our feelings about having a baby together. Please guide us to the right decision for us and our future child." Here you may call upon any higher power that you believe in: God, Angels, Universal Energy, etc. according to your belief system or you may simply finish the statement of intentionality as written. I suggest something very simple, such as, "Please, God, hear our prayer." Or "May the Angels be with us and bless us." Or "We wish to be guided by the Divine (Universal) Plan".

A good physical position to do this exercise in is to lie together in the spoon position on your bed or couch. Both of you lie on your sides, facing the same direction, with the woman in front of the man. Put on some relaxing music and attempt to focus on your intention to have a baby. The woman might put her hands over her abdomen and her partner might also put his hand or hands over her abdomen. Now, the next part is so incredibly simple that you may doubt that it will work. You simply ask yourself (not each other, but yourself) if you are ready to have a baby with your partner. And you wait and quietly listen to the music. Any of the quiet, relaxing New Age type music is good or classical music – in any case it should be something soothing, without lyrics, but with a positive, balancing feel to it.

The answer will come to you either the first time you do this exercise or after a few times. You will know when it is the right time to begin trying to have a baby together. This realization may come to you through a bodily sensation, with a thought or an emotion or feeling. Perhaps the answer won't appear right away, but be alert in the next few days after the experience. There are many ways that guidance may come to you, even after the meditative experience. You may start to be aware of seeing many pregnant women or babies, or you may hear a song or open a book that may bring you the answer you seek.

If you receive a negative response, it is best to accept the response and to continue working on yourselves and the relationship. In fact, there may be nothing more that you can do, as the soul that will inhabit the body of your baby must also be ready to be born. I very much believe in "Divine Timing", so once you've done all you can do, patience is the answer. I would advise you to repeat the exercise every few months or so and also to discuss your negative response with each other. Could it be that one of you is afraid to have a baby? Are you sure of your desire? Of your partner? Of the stability of your relationship? Have you healed sufficiently from your past? These are all questions to be considered.

When you receive an affirmative answer it is time to move ahead with the following exercise for actually welcoming a Star child into your womb. In this exercise, you open to higher energies and send a signal out to the Universal Mind that you are willing and ready to share the love that you have together with another person.

Exercise for welcoming the birth of a Star child:
Again, this is a rather simplistic exercise, but it can be very powerful. It should be done only once, though it can be repeated in six months, should you not become pregnant within that time.

Sit facing each other on the floor or on cushions with your legs crossed in front of you. Those of you who are very agile may sit facing each other with your legs open in a "v" form. The woman can then put her legs on top of the man's. You may join hands, if you like, which will form a circle. If you wish, you may put a candle or another object on the floor between you. This can be a symbol of the baby you are inviting to join you. It is best to choose an object, which is "charged" with meaning, such as a stone you found together, a crystal, something which represents your familial ties, or any other object which you cherish.

Now the stage is set.

Imagine that you are surrounded by a loving golden light that is warm and safe. This light is all around you and your partner – it is part of the love that you feel for each other. Imagine that you open your heart and send out the love within you to your partner. You are opening to Divine Love and you feel your heart space growing larger and larger. You feel your body opening, the top of your head – you are with your partner and you know that this is safe.

Now, imagine that there is a golden beam of light shining down into the circle, which you have formed with your arms and legs. This is a light that comes from far away in the universe. It can also be a color that you love. Imagine that there are golden sparks of light, like little stars, pouring down to Earth. And now within that stream of light, imagine a baby filled with light coming down to Earth between the two of you. Allow your heart and your bodies to open to this new fragile being. Send it all the love, light, and peace that you can. Tell your baby that you welcome her, that you can create a safe loving environment for him. And continue to send love.

Imagine that the baby's energy enters into your bodies and into your hearts, that she or he is a part of you already, that the birth has already taken place. Take your time to enjoy this happy moment, this feeling of joy and the sharing of love.

When you feel complete, you can open your eyes and look deeply into your partner's eyes. And remember to say thank you to your baby who will arrive at the perfect moment according to the Divine Plan. When you feel like it, you can share the experience with one another or just sit quietly together until you feel like sharing. And whenever you feel the experience has come to a natural end, you may blow out the candle if you used one. If you have a little altar set up in your house, you may choose to put the candle or symbolic object there. If not, you may choose to put the object in a safe place or on your nightstand by your bed.

By the way, an altar is always a very nice addition to any home and it provides a place for you to pray, meditate, unwind, relax, or just think. More about that in Part II, Chapter Seven.

Because there are many fine books on pregnancy and the birthing process, I will not include that information here. Some things that you should be aware or check into are the following: the effects of ultra sound viewing on the unborn baby; vaccinations and problems resulting from them; food allergies and environmental sensitivities; and methods of birthing including those under water, natural home child births. By the way, in some countries, though not the United States, it is considered perfectly normal to have a home birth – for example in Holland where most babies are born at home.

In my research, it is interesting to note that people under hypnosis have reported pre-birth, embryonic memories. This means that whatever happens during pregnancy may be registered somewhere in your baby's memory. One more reason why it is important to clear out your negative patterns before getting pregnant. Also, singing or playing the same song over and over while pregnant and then immediately after birth seems to lessen the trauma of birth. I recently treated a pregnant friend of mine whose baby actually demanded music be played to her. We weren't sure if the choice of music, which was from India, was to benefit the baby directly or the mother, who happened to have been born there.

You may want to know how to determine the best music for your baby. I use a simple method where the mother-to-be places one hand on her stomach over the baby and the other on my shoulder. Then I look at or touch the CD's or cassettes available. And the ones that make my body feel strong or that "seem" stronger in vibration than the others are the ones I propose. However, don't despair if you do not have anyone close to you with this possibility. You can do it yourself. Play a few of your favorite selections, while sitting or lying quietly, and feel the reaction of your baby and of your own body. Whatever feels good and soothing for you will surely be right for your baby.

As far as I can tell, the most important aspect of the musical experience is that you play the same piece or sing the same song repetitively. In this way, the baby comes to recognize the melody as something soothing and familiar. You may play the music all during the pregnancy, but it is especially meaningful during the last trimester when everyone agrees the baby has the capacity to hear and respond to noises. In fact, I recently read that at six weeks of gestation the internal ear has begun to develop and at eight weeks the external ear has formed. So on with the music!

And remember, if all this advice and these suggestions add to your tension about having a child, discard them! In my opinion, the main ingredient in having a successful pregnancy is the love that you have for your baby and for each other. If you love your baby, things usually work out okay. It is important not to follow everything you read because this would be overwhelming. Whatever feels right for you, will be just perfect for your baby. Trust is so important in raising a child or in any new adventure because we never know the outcome. Why didn't our parents ever tell us to take risks, have fun and do what we want?

Why couldn't we all have had Deepak Chopra as our father? He told his children from the beginning that they were on Earth for a reason and that they had to find out for themselves. He taught them to meditate and told them that he didn't want them to focus on doing well in school! They shouldn't think about getting the best grades or worry about going to the best colleges. He told them to focus on how they could serve humanity and to discover what their unique talents were[33]. It is interesting to note that with this guidance, all his children made top grades, went to fine schools, became successful in the world, and are happy! Well, I agree with him -- more about this in the upcoming chapters about raising a Star child.

Chapter Seven:

The World of Adult Star Children

If my theory is correct that Star children have been around for a very long time, then some of us are part of the baby boom and have already passed the half-century mark. Others are young adults, very often parents to this "new" wave of children that are coming now. To me, this makes a lot of sense, as the new children are of a very high vibration and need parents of finer energy, thus they are choosing to incarnate in families where one or both parents are Star children themselves. One researcher reports that he has worked with a family of four generations of Star children and surely many of us are about to become or already are grandparents to Star children.

Although this book and many others are written about specific groups of children, I must say that I don't consider myself or any of the other Star children that I have met to be "special". Star children will feel special and superior to others only if adults choose to see them that way. Every child, every person should be encouraged to fulfill his or her mission on Earth, use his or her talents to the fullest, and be a meaningful part of society. Who is to say that the man I buy my vegetables from is not more evolved than someone who writes "spiritual" books? Who's to measure the impact of one human being on Earth?

The beauty of identifying with Star people is that those of you who feel alone suddenly can have a shared experience. There are others like you and me out there. We are not alone. Sure, our beliefs and abilities even within this group identity vary greatly, but we have a common bond, a way of speaking to each other, which is like short hand. Many of us have taken a path that is far from the beaten one – we are marching to a different drummer as they say. Others of us have chosen to have normal jobs and to contribute to society from within. One is not better than the other, it all depends on what role we have opted for this time.

While our different point of view and expectations can cause us a lot of grieve and pain, we can also rejoice in them. As we mature, we learn to accept ourselves, our gifts and our limitations, just like everyone else. We know what it's like to not "fit into society" and we learned this at an early age. We didn't have the same interests as our peers and we often felt lonely and isolated. However, as time goes on, we are finding more and more of our Star family members; and this brings us such joy.

It seems that as Earth energy and consciousness moves up, a great many people are moving further and further away from their birth families. Some of us spent our entire lifetimes trying to fit into a birth family that was giving us a message of how to be and act, which did not coincide with who we really are. We are the ones who are a bit "different" from other family members. Recently, my older brother stood up at his daughter's wedding, which I officiated at as the minister by the way, and said that he finally was beginning to understand what I'd been trying to tell him all along. Ah, recognition is sweet after more than fifty years of feeling crazy!

Many Star people are in the process of what I call "breaking familial codes". Each family has a "secret code", a way of interacting, which can be very subtle. For example, parents expect their children to have the same values, often equivalent levels of education, and of course a certain way of behaving. The child who varies from these "norms" either in childhood or adulthood breaks these familial codes. Many of us are in the process of identifying the messages that we received, or may still be receiving, in our family and we are learning to accept or reject them. We were "different" as children and people around us did not understand or even know what to do with us. We were the ugly ducklings who have grown into the beautiful swans. Life, as we age, seems to get more agreeable.

What's a simple way to break familial codes or messages?

One simple way to break negative familial messages, often given to you inadvertently, is to sit quietly and ask to focus on one message that you received and don't want to keep anymore. Then quietly, you can address that person directly in a meditation and say, *"(Mother, Father, etc.), you gave me this message: You are . . . (fill in the blank). I no longer accept it as my truth and instead I now give myself a new message in its place: I am . . . (fill in the blank)."* Then you give yourself a positive message.

Here's an example: *"(Mom, Dad, etc.), you gave me this message: You are worthless. I no longer accept it as my truth, instead I give myself this new message: I am a valuable and loving person."*

Notice in the above example when you state the message you were given, you state it as if someone is speaking to you, using the "you" form of address. Remember to use this wording, "You gave me this message: *YOU are* worthless." Don't use the wording, "You gave me this message: *I am* worthless." Keep the message with the person who gave it to you. This is very important because you want to break the code and not accept the message as your truth on any level, especially in the subconscious.

Then note well that with the newly substituted message, you use the "I" form of address because you want to own the new message. For instance, "*I am a valuable and loving person*." You want it to become a part of you. The positive new message which you have given yourself should be read when you wake up in the morning and before going to sleep each night for at least a month. It takes time and effort to break familial codes and the work is ongoing.

The good news is that the more you let go of your birth family, the more apt you are to "run into" members of your Star family. Of course, most of you will always want to stay in close contact with your birth family. I am close to mine and speak to my mother almost every week, even though we live half the world apart. And I believe that as we get wiser all friends and family usually become increasingly more important.

Meeting members of your Star Family

Finding Star family members is exhilarating and exciting. How many times have you just known someone? I remember over a year ago walking into the home of J.C., whom I'd never met before. When I saw him, the first thought I had was "Oh there you are. I wondered when you'd show up." It just seemed so natural and easy and not only have we become good "e-friends", but also I have in a way become part of his extended family. An "e-friend" is someone you rarely see in physical form, but send e-mails to on a regular basis. This encounter is just one small example and we all have them. These people are part of our Star family.

I believe that we reincarnate in clusters and that there are certain "hook-ups" that we make throughout our lives. My son was an obvious one for me, as he served as my spiritual teacher in the physical form during the ten short years that he was on Earth. Hook-ups or connections strengthen us; we find that we are not alone, that we have brothers and sisters and even people who re-parent us in our Star family constellation. I believe that we meet each other because we *need* each other. Every time a connection is made, the whole network of world servers becomes stronger.

Sometimes, people ask me how they can speed up or increase their chances of meeting members of their Star families. In my opinion, it is a question of evolution on the part of both parties. When you both reach a certain realization level, you will meet. For instance, you may visit the same city and know the same people for years, when suddenly someone says, "Oh you should meet a certain person." And then, that's it; you meet someone you already "know". The mystery door opens and its magic begins.

I remember meeting a now very good friend of mine who lives in a remote village of France. I am from near San Francisco, California and, in fact, I'd never been to such a village before. It was hidden away, with one little cobbled stone pedestrian path and no stores! Imagine! The chances of my meeting her, if calculated statistically, are practically non-existent, yet it happened. Anne-Marie and I often laugh about this as I sit by the fireplace in her snug little home in a place where time stands still. It is so wonderful to discover your Star family every where in the world living in all different circumstances.

With members of your Star family, you can finally "connect" with someone actually on the Earth. You can gain a lot of strength just knowing that there are others with similar belief systems. It is always nice to meet "an old friend". And those of you that are young adults, you have the possibility of meeting your Star family at an earlier age as the whole process speeds up. One image that I like very much is this: "Having higher dimensional beings coming to Earth is like putting your cake mixer on high speed instead of low speed. It whips things up faster and transforms a bunch of ingredients into something new and different!"[34].

Also, be aware that as you start to open and raise your vibrations, you will begin to see others of like vibrations everywhere. I don't know if these people are Star children or not – remember there is no one who can say whether someone is a Star child or not. It is for each person to decide that for him or herself. An example: one day I arrived in Holland at the train station with a very heavy suitcase. At the head of the train was the conductor who smiled and pointed the way. Then I saw the escalator and as I was getting on it, an old woman turned and smiled. She "recognized" me with her inner soul eye. I have had this type of help all over the world. I don't know what's going on exactly, but I can tell you there is a group of people here on Earth who have come with a specific mission to bring peace and who recognize each other. When you meet someone from the same vibration, you know the person. The Star child vibration is just one of the many colors from a rainbow of all humans. There are many peace-loving people here – all of us working to bring about friendly relationships and help each other whenever we can.

Becoming our "real selves"

Becoming what I call your Star self is your "real" work here on Earth and our Star mission is to love one another and help in the peacemaking process. You and I are learning to express ourselves in the most authentic way possible. We are learning to become our "real selves". I have already written a book about this process, but because it has been published in Dutch only, I would like to share a few ideas that are in it.

I believe that we are programmed before birth and equipped with everything we need to live our Earth life. We know who we are and why we are coming to Earth, what our mission is. Once we are born, we fall into forgetfulness due to the denseness of Earth energy and become Earthbound, often with a focus on Earthly success and achievement. Then we experience a crisis or receive an insight that causes our forgetful state to shatter and radically change. Fear, shock, pain, and an inability to function can accompany this period. We then begin to put everything back together again in a more authentic way in order to experience self-awareness and eventually total integration. Many of the younger Star children will not have to experience the crisis period as they are falling less profoundly into the state of forgetfulness.

The more you conform to society's norms, the further you are from your authentic path. The idea is to be yourself, to touch the outer edges of your being, of your capacities and to not feel safe and secure in everything you do. Instead of telling us to be careful, our parents should have told us to take risks, to try everything, to do what we want. Each moment of existence we are choosing life or death. Every time you choose something out of fear of the future, or of the past repeating itself, you are choosing to die a little. You must determine what you want and don't want, and then take action. Armchair faith won't work! I could sit and believe that I can write books for the rest of my life, but if I don't pick up paper and pen and start, nothing will be accomplished. We need to practice what is called *active faith*.

For instance, I have met people who tell me they want to work. I ask them if they have their resume ready, along with letters of references. Have they invested in clothing suitable for the position they are seeking? Even if they have very little money, they can still shop at the used clothing stores and put together a decent outfit. So many people sit at home dreaming when they should be "digging their ditches". After all, how can abundance flow in our lives if we don't do our part?

When you follow your heart's desires, you become strong and authentic. You begin to take responsibility for the circumstances in your life and at that point you become "real". It is as if we are ships at sea and until a certain point we can be blown off course by other people's expectations, advice and desires. After we have been at sea for a while as captain of our own ship, it would take a very strong "wind" to throw us off course.

Each of us longs to follow the pathway of our hearts, and not societal or mental dictates. When you begin to give expression to your authentic desires, you begin to feel safe, secure, and accepted because you are the only one that can give yourself those gifts. The only difference between some of you and me, is that I dare to look foolish, to fail, and more importantly to succeed. *It is always easier to stand safely in a crowd than to become who you really are.*

Flexibility and curiosity are needed in large doses to do this individual life mission work, but what choice do you have? If you want to feel joyful as a child, alive with energy, then reaching out, spreading your wings is obligatory! *You can't fly until you leap off the cliff, and that leap in faith makes all the difference in the world.* To begin the process of opening your heart, you must first love and reassure yourself that you are loved and protected in the world.

One of my favorite things to tell people is "you can be the Star that you are". It is such a hopeful message and so true. We must work to let go of our past, to break familial codes, to go within ourselves and to touch that place of authenticity. It is from our inner Star that we will find our way. This is our small flame that we have brought to Earth. When we shine the smallest light in even the darkest room, we can find our way. You must pursue your heart's desires, your soul's longings in a radical way, taking time for yourself to be all you can be in order to give, be and express the best **you** possible for everyone on Earth. Each time you grow, each time you smile, each time you join with someone, all of humanity rejoices. It is by remaining balanced, centered and in communication with your soul's desires that you are able to rest joyfully on the Earth plane.

I believe our inner Star is always connected with a Divine Source. You cannot imagine an ocean without at the same time imagining the water of which it is composed. It is the same with all creation. Everyone and everything is part of creation, and it is therefore impossible that anything can be missing or absent. There is the basic ingredient, if you will, of which every thing and every one is composed. You can think of this as love energy, which is always present. Each of you is an individual expression of the whole, the One, just as the beams of the sun are the sun, yet any one individual beam could not be called the entire sun. Just as the ocean is made up of billions upon billions of drops of water, so is the sun composed of an infinite number of light beams. Drop by drop, the ocean is made and the sun as well.

How can you stay connected to your Star essence?

In order to stay consciously connected to your Star self, it is good to take a few moments upon arising and before sleeping to sit quietly and imagine that you are in a golden light. Calmly see that light in you, all around you and covering everything. The light is the Life Force of which you are a part. You may also visualize a shaft of light coming from the sun in the morning or the stars at night descending down through and around you, flowing into the ground. This can be experienced as a symbol of your connection. Both of these simple exercises can also be used throughout the day, especially when you are not sure of what to do next, when you have to make a decision, or whenever you feel out of balance. Just close your eyes, sit quietly, and imagine the light. It works very well and will help you make choices from a deeper, more balanced space.

Many Star children have asked me what can they do to bring greater peace on Earth and thus fulfill their Star mission. I believe that it is through living our values, honoring ourselves and others and helping each other that peace will be ultimately achieved.

Once in meditation, I asked the same question about the furtherance of peace on Earth. In the following material, which to me summarizes what we are doing here, the bridge stands as a symbol between the physical world and the spiritual one, or one may say between the Earth Star and your Star of Origin. Here's the information that I received:

Join hands with your brothers and sisters. Help each other. Be kind. Be soft. Be the love that you are. Hold each other's hands. The bridge's steps can be damp and slippery at times. Don't let go. Don't let anyone fall. And if they do, go to them and offer comfort. Put your arms around them. Send them all the healing energy that you can. Imagine them perfect and safe, surrounded by light. Be gentle with each other. Offer your love, your support, your positive thoughts, and your uplifting words. Say a little prayer to help your sister or brother. Forgive those who attack you. Send them a bouquet of loving thoughts instead.

Stand up for what you know to be true. Be courageous. Be Brave. Live what you talk about. Live your beliefs. Stand fully in your life. Express your uniqueness. Share your gifts. Lift up your sisters and brothers.

Spread joy and happiness around liberally. It doesn't cost anything and it can buy so much for a suffering friend. Hold the last candle in the darkest night for your companion. Offer encouragement. Tell your sister that she is the most incredible, unique human being that there ever was or will be. Sit with your brother when all appears lost. Encourage him to continue the path, the journey, the search.

Assure each other that heaven is possible on Earth. Be thankful for each day, each hour of life. Thank those around you for the gifts they bear, whether they be diamonds or hard lessons which are just diamonds in the rough.

And finally, love each other like there's no tomorrow. Live as if each moment were your last. And laugh with all the joy of the universe. The stars are waiting for you to shine. The Angels are waiting for you to fly. The lion is waiting for you to roar. The heavens are opening up to welcome you home. Come a little closer now. Listen, listen carefully now:

You are a Star. Everyone is a Star in his or her own life. Many of you still think that it is "spiritual" to not be all that you can be. You spend time and energy worrying about other people and trying to fix them. The most "spiritual" aspect of a human life is to express the God given talents that you have. Each person has a space to fill – this space is ever expanding. There are no edges to your being because you are part of the Infinite Whole.

When you fulfill your life mission, you are naturally becoming closer to the Source of what you are. This is why you are being encouraged to be the Star that you are! Now, some of you may think that it is egotistical to think in terms of becoming "a Star"! What is meant here is that each of you have a leading role to play in your own life – and most of you are playing a supporting role, and some of you haven't even come on stage yet.

When you know who you are and what you are to do, you must do it, not only for yourself, but for everyone. As soon as you take your leading role – fulfilling what you came here to do – others can more easily relate to you. When no one is clear about who you are, how can they clearly interact with you? As long as you are not clear about what you want, how can another give it to you? You must be quiet and meditate. Know what you want and who you are. Then, the Whole Universe will work with you, will support you, and will become the stage for your life.

You are a Star. Be who you are."

The last thing I would like to say to you, dear Star sisters and brothers, is that you are not alone. I have "found" you with this book and there are those around you offering their love and support. The network has begun and there's no breaking the intricately woven web that we have so consciously spun. No matter how greatly you long to go back to your Star, the portals have been closed. We may be sad, we may yearn to return to our Stars, but for us, our work is right here, right now. Let's remember why we have come, join together, and complete our mission so that Planet Earth will someday experience all the love and joy that we once knew in the Light.

In order to raise the vibrations of everyone to a peaceful level, we must be Warriors of Light and Love. Please read the next little satirical theatrical sketch with this in mind. It is a reminder to all of us that we must be active peacemakers. When we connect with the Love force within us with the intention of co-creating a peaceful world, we will succeed!

Prologue

(The curtains open. The stage is empty. One Star child stands front and center.)

Star Child: *There is a sounding of the trumpet for all humankind to go within, to listen and follow their guidance and intuition. And finally, to join together both physically and spiritually to bring peace to Earth, a loving lasting peace.*

(Enter Star children and adults of every size, shape, and color)

Dialogue

Star children are singing, laughing, joining hands – in other words, having fun. (A rough voice off stage plays the role of "World" which represents the current state of world consciousness.)

World: *Wait a minute. Stop! So who are you anyway and what are you doing singing and dancing about?*

Star Children: *Oh, we are the Star children. We've come to Earth from distant stars.*

World: *Stop right there! You expect me to believe that you've come here from stars. You've got to be kidding!*

Star Children: *Well, no, we are serious. Listen for a moment. We remember our stars – that's what makes it hard for us because on our stars we experienced living in harmony, peace, and love.*

World: *You're dreaming. There's no place like that. You're just naive children anyway. What do you know?*

Star Children: *We know a lot about peace. In fact, it's very difficult for most of us to live here on Earth. We often want to go back to our stars. Sometimes, we know things and see things that others don't.*

And we feel alone. It's not easy here, believe us.

World: *Oh, so I'm not good enough for you. Your whole group sounds like a bunch of spiritual elitists. Why don't you just be normal? Then everything would be fine.*

Star Children: *What do you mean "be normal"! We don't want to be competitive, judgmental, aggressive, and filled with doubt like most people on Earth. What we're saying is this: We remember another way and we can help bring peace to Earth. We are like peace messengers. We can help.*

World: *Oh, you just think you're special. It's not my problem if you have trouble being here. If you'd give up all your stupid ideas about those others stars, you wouldn't have any trouble.*

Star Children: *You don't understand. We don't want to be different. We just are different. We are more sensitive than a lot of people. All kinds of things can bother us, like bright lights, loud noises, odors, and even food! Many of us long to go back to our real homes where people lived in peace and harmony. We feel we don't belong here on Earth. It can be too hard to be inside a body.*

World: *So desensitize yourselves, for God's sake. Stop being so weak and sensitive. You are causing all your own problems. Toughen up.*

Star Children: *That's just it! We can't. Everyone and everything on Earth has a certain energy vibration. All Star children have the same one. We have to have this lighter vibration in order to remember who we are and what our peace mission is. Don't you want to be a peaceful world?*

World: *Well, sure, but that would take a miracle.*

Star Children: *Why don't you understand? If you allow us to be different, accept us for who we are, we can help make the miracle of peace present on Earth.*

World: *Know what – I'm tired of all this talk about peace. I think you'd better just leave it to the grown ups – the politicians, government leaders, the important people. They'll figure it out. Now, go to school or to your jobs. Keep your mouths shut and do as you are told.*

Star Children: *(silence)*

World: *Yet another threat to peace has been squashed.*

Star Children – smiling, singing, and holding hands – sing the following song:

We are the Star Children

Peace makers of tomorrow

Glints of energy dancing on oceans

Across every continent we come

To say: "We love you! And

Love one another."

References:

1. Internet site: http://www.drunvalo.net
2. Encyclopedia Britannica
3. Internet site: http://www.drunvalo.net
4. Carroll, Lee and Tober, Jan. Indigo Children, Hay House, 1999, p.1. (Contains excellent references in the Endnotes.)
5. Ibid., Tappe, Nancy Ann, "Introduction to the Indigos", interviewed by Jan Tober, pgs. 6-17.
6. Cabobianco, Flavio. Je Viens du Soliel. (French edition), Editions St. Michel, 1992, p. 46.
7. Dennis, Caryl and Whitman Parker, The Millennium Children, Rainbows Unlimited, 1997, p. 266.
8. Cabobianco, p. 14.
9. Dennis, p. 200.
10. Creelman, Candice. "All You Need is Love: The Indigo Experience," in Indigo Children, p. 212.
11. Boylan, Dr. Richard, "Star Kids Benefit From Special Schooling", Internet.
12. Dennis, p. 201.
13. Ibid., p. 201.
14. Cababianco, p. 54
15. Lauren, Phoebe, Star Child, unpublished English manuscript, 1996.
16. Rowling, J.K., Harry Potter and the Sorcerer's Stone, Scholastic Inc., 1999.
17. Internet site: http://www.jps.net.drboylan
18. Cababianco, p. 15.
19. Catherine at Internet site: http://litespirit.com
20. Randles, Jenny, Star Children: The True Story of Alien Offspring Among Us, Sterling Publishing Co., 1995, pgs. 207-208 (Appendix).
21. Internet site: http://www.crystalinks.com/starseeds.html
22. Internet site: http://www.jps.net.drboylan/strknrpt.htm
23. Internet site: http://www.jps.net/drboylan/skccdna.htm
24. Gershom, Rabbi Yonassan, Beyond the Ashes – Cases of Reincarnation from the Holocaust, ARE Press, 1992, pgs. 242-3.
25. Cababianco, p. 38.
26. Catherine at http://litespirit.com
27. Cabobianco, p. 14.
28. Wambach, Helen, quoted in Dennis, Caryl, The Millenium Children, pgs. 268-269.
29. Ibid., p. 269.

30. Cabobianco, p.17.
31. Carroll, pgs. 95-100. Also see Internet site: www.Indigochild.com.
32. Mayhew, Mary, Your Star Child, 21st Century Books, 1996. Internet site: http://www.marymayhew.com
33. Chopra, Deepak, The Seven Spiritual Laws of Success, Amber-Allen Publishing, 1994, pgs. 96-96.
34. Internet site: http://litespirit.com

STAR CHILDREN Among us

Part 2

> "The art of spiritually approaching the child, from whom we are so far, is a secret that can establish human brotherhood, it is a divine art that will lead to the peace of mankind. The children are so many, they are numberless, they are not one star, they are more like the Milky Way, that stream of stars that passes right across the heavens"

Marie Montessori 1939

Part Two:

Introduction

How can we "catch a falling Star and keep it close and never let it fade away"? Some Star children pass through our lives only briefly, while others linger for a while, but all of them stay in our hearts forever. What can we teach those who come to us and what can we learn from them?

In Part Two of this publication, the focus is on what attributes and values can we help our Star child embody. We will explore together some of the following questions: How can we work together with our child and encourage kindness, love and a sense of community without diminishing each child's uniqueness? What does it mean to accept our Star child exactly as he or she is? What is the proper role of a parent? What happens when we allow our children to become authority figures? How can we protect Star children from incompatible vibrations? How can we encourage a Star child to honor his or her gifts while not considering the child special? How can we help our child remain balanced, functioning in the world, yet still connected to his or her deep inner knowledge? How can a Star child connect to the stars and to other Star children and adults? How can we remain hopeful that peace will become a reality in a still violent world?

For those of you that are adult Star children, Part II will help you understand current problems you may be having as a Star child. The following material is not only valuable for raising and working with Star children, but it can serve to heal your inner child, to understand your past experiences, and to enhance balance in your everyday life.

There are a myriad of issues to look at in raising a Star child. I consider Part Two to be a very limited attempt to answer some of these questions. I have still many more questions than responses. The more I conduct research about Star children, the more gray areas there are and the less sure I am of my findings. What follows are my initial impressions, all subject to change as I, myself, evolve and as the situation clarifies itself. Of one thing I am certain, there are Star children on Earth and they are here to help us. As for the rest, well, I hope you will read on.

Chapter One:
Be There And Care

Certainly, we all know that children are like flowers, some more delicate than others. We also know that all children have the possibility to flourish, given enough love and care. So some of what I am about to write will apply to all children everywhere. However, my focus is specifically on Star children and how you as parents, friends, family members, educators, or therapists can help the Star child blossom.

Remember also, that you can "self-parent" and apply everything that follows to yourself. So if you did not receive what you required from authority figures in your life, you can always give yourself that gift now. As you read, you can *imagine* that you are receiving all the guidance, love and acceptance that you needed. Just pause every once in a while, close your eyes, and imagine yourself as a child. Then imagine receiving whatever you did not actually receive as a child. The imagination is a very powerful inner resource, which we all have.

Being kind and gentle with these children is really the only choice you have. If you are not, they will close up tight and may not ever open up again. In general, they have a very low tolerance for unkindness and are easily hurt. Star children are able to detect unkind thoughts, are often able to see anger in people's auras, and they react especially strong to any unkindness that is directed towards them.

At an early age, they expect to be treated like an equal and when you talk down to them, use baby talk or have a condescending voice, they can be easily insulted. If you negate their knowing or their feelings, again they can feel affronted. For example, when they "see" something that others don't see, it is important to enter into their world as much as you are able. *Being kind, you can simply be more accepting of what they are experiencing*.

You do not like it when you share something with a friend and she tells you to forget about it as if what you are sharing has little importance. It is the same for the Star child. The only difference is that they will often tell you things that you imagine to be impossible. This is where your kindness and acceptance comes in.

Here's an example that might help. One day my son, Marcus, saw the color red in his father's aura when he came home from work. Marcus quickly picked up his homework and went upstairs, saying, "Uh-oh, I'm getting out of here. I'm going up to my room!"

I followed him and asked what was wrong. He told me what he saw and that the color red meant that his father was angry. At the time, I knew very little about auras, and although I did ask him questions about what he saw, I told him that his father was in a perfectly good mood and that he need not worry. In other words, I negated his reality. I also told him that I expected him to come down and eat dinner as usual.

Of course, at the dinner table his father suddenly became very angry and Marcus just looked at me and left the table. While I tried to always be kind and gentle with Marcus, it was only much later that I understood his level of sensitivity. So, being kind means making room for difference and sometimes that requires a lot of room!

If I had had the opportunity of reading this book when rearing Marcus, I would have reacted differently to his concern. I would have acknowledged that what he saw was real for him, and I may have even asked him more questions about his perceptions. I might then have said something like this, "Yes, I can only imagine what you see and how you must feel. It must be difficult seeing colors around people and knowing things that others don't know. Right now, however, your father doesn't seem to be angry, and I'd still like you to come down to dinner when I call you." Now, I have been kind in every aspect. I acknowledge his knowing and his different way of being, and brought my reality into it. Finally, because we were a family, I still require him to come to dinner.

While we want to be kind and understanding of our children's differences, we must also help them realize that they have to function in this world as much as possible. I do not believe in allowing these children to dictate how the whole family should function; yet I do believe we must allow them to have their own reality.

As an example, I know Star children who literally take over whole households, telling others what they should and should not do. Of course this can happen only when you, as parents, relinquish your rightful role as guide for your child. Remember that your children may indeed possess "higher universal knowledge", yet haven't a clue how to function on Earth!

The following are examples of what may occur when the child assumes the dominant role in a family. A child may require the whole family to meditate together or not to talk to a certain person. They may forbid relatives from visiting and refuse to go on visits. They may require people to take their shoes off when entering the house, not allow anyone in certain parts of the house, and become very upset when their ideas and rules are not followed. Yes, I have seen some pretty unusual behavior.

Here's a more concrete example: Star children may dictate what the family may eat and even what time the meals should be served. If your child chooses to follow a restricted diet and be a vegetarian, when no one else in your family is one, that's great. However, if someone else in the family chooses to eat a more "normal" meal at the table, that is also acceptable and the child must learn to tolerate all people. After all, if they have come as peacemakers, then turning up their noses at what other people eat can hardly contribute to their mission.

I have also been to lovely homes and centers where everyone is vegetarian and all who eat there follow the same diet, which is perfectly normal. Here, I am speaking about a situation where a child is allowed to dictate to an entire group of people what they are allowed or not to eat. Just as you are kind to your Star child, you must point out gently when he or she is being intolerant. We must never forget, as parents, your child may have a higher vibration and a greater sensitivity than you do, and *he or she is still a child, needing parents for guidance!*

I have noticed that many Star children have peculiar eating habits; being vegetarian is the 'tip of the iceberg', so to speak. There are children that eat only one thing; others who will eat only plainly prepared food, some will use huge amounts of a condiment, and some that refuse to eat altogether.

I have met Star children, especially teenaged girls, that are anorexic and slowly committing suicide because they want to go "back to their star". Some children are afraid of certain foods because of its color, origin or texture. Again, here we have to be patient and understanding. Sometimes, of course, we must also get them professional help. I will talk more about how we can help them adjust to being here on Earth later in the book.

I shall never forget Rabbi Gelberman's wise words when I was studying to become an interfaith minister at The New Seminary in New York City. He said, "Never forget, always 'in addition to', never 'instead of'". This is a very valuable bit of advice when interacting with your child. He or she may insist that something is out and out wrong, like eating animals or even trimming a bush. Our job as guides is to agree that for right now it is the child's belief that this or that practice is wrong AND other people have difference beliefs.

Star children can often have very high principles and may wish to "inflict" them on others. This can make life difficult for them and unpleasant for those around them. When a Star child believes something, it is good to point out that not everyone sees things in the same way. The Star child's knowing, in other words, is to be honored when possible for the child, but not necessarily considered right for everyone around.

Star children can be very seductive in their beliefs because they are usually of the highest nature. Fortunately, most of them are aware of the fact that everyone on Earth is at a difference level of evolution. Although most Star children are well adjusted, it is good to be prepared in advance for these types of situations that may arise.

How can we be kind and still draw the line? The easiest and perhaps most effective way, is to take the child aside and explain to him or her that while you agree he or she is entitled to his or her beliefs, not everyone thinks or feels the same way. Thus, we can tell them that when they are in public and interacting with others it is best to keep these ideas quiet.

Please do not misunderstand me here, this does not imply that you are diminishing their beliefs or negating them in any way. You are attempting to teach them appropriate, acceptable behavior, which in the long run will make life easier for them. However, this message must be clearly given or the child may believe you disapprove of their beliefs or abilities and he or she may begin to withdraw. You can also explain, for example, that you have beliefs and ideas that are private as well, and that we do not say everything we think or feel to each other.

In order to keep the communication open with your Star child however, you must assure and reassure her or him that you are open to hear everything and anything he or she wants to tell you, because you will always try to understand. You do not want your child to close down, yet you also know that he or she must interact with others in a friendly, kind way.

By sharing your feelings, thoughts, and experience, in a kind open manner, you are also **being honest** with your child and this, above all else, is an absolute requirement when interacting with Star children. Don't ever pretend that you see something that you don't see or that something seems perfectly normal when it doesn't. If you are tired, angry, frustrated, or haven't a moment to spare, it is better to be honest. These children know immediately if you are lying or humoring them and their confidence in you will be eroded. In other words, they know what's behind the words of their parents.

For example, if your child sees auras or little beings around plants and you don't, then you must say so. You may say something like this, *"Oh, I'm so happy that you are able to see . . . (whatever) and I wish I could too, but I don't. What do you think those little beings are doing? or What do you think those colors mean? or When you see the color (name the color) what do you feel?"* Certainly, you say you are happy they are seeing these things only if you really are happy. If, on the other hand, you feel concerned or frightened by what they see you can voice that as well. Of course, if the child is frightened by what she or he has seen, then you go into your role as parent and comfort the child and you do not share your fear for the time being. Most of this is common sense, yet it is good to have a bit of preparation before these things occur.

Being honest is part of **being genuine**. When we are genuine we can be ourselves. I have seen parents trying to be perfect for their children. There are parents who would not dare do things that their children disapprove, even though they long to do so; some of these children have very unusual beliefs.

One little girl refused to go into a certain store because it had "dark things" in it. After a period of time, all the members of the family stopped going into the store. This meant traveling more than a half hour each way to another town every week. The store, unfortunately, was the only grocery store in their small village. Being genuine and following your own beliefs would mean doing your grocery shopping there like every other family in your village – unless, of course, you feel agitated by going in the store. However, you could acknowledge that your daughter sees "dark things" in the store and honor her belief by not making her go into it.

So there is a pattern emerging here with the following steps:

1. We acknowledge the Star child's belief as being correct for her or him.
2. We acknowledge that we are all different and that we can't impose our beliefs on each other (always "in addition", never "instead of").
3. We help the child to function in the world by continuing to guide him or her and not relinquishing our roles as parents (after all, there is a reason why your child chose you).

Flexibility is another quality that can be useful in interacting with Star children. Their extreme sensitivity practically requires it. I remember that when I was a young girl I used to have horrible nightmares. The theme was always the same: the bad men were coming to get me and take me away. This, I believe, had to do with my past life where I was killed in a concentration camp during WWII. Anyway, my mother and father were very wise. They tried a number of things to help me, including giving me a bit of sugar before bed; looking under the bed and all around the room before I went to sleep; teaching me how to enter into my dreams and defeat the "bad guys"; and finally, if I had a nightmare showed me how I could turn my pillow over to the "good dream" side.

This is one example of caring, flexible parents and the openness that is required. I don't know if they would have taken me to a past life regression therapist if they had had knowledge of one. The point is that when your child is "different", you must be flexible and able to respond to those differences, whether they are belief systems or unusual perceptions or downright bizarre experiences. You must have confidence in your own intuition and decision-making process as to when you can handle the situation and when you need to consult someone who has more knowledge than you do.

As parents, we must remain hopeful that our child will find his or her way in the world. We must not throw up our hands and label the child in a negative way. As long as we can have hope for our children and hope to find solutions to their problems, they themselves will remain optimistic about attaining their ultimate goal of peace. By now, you are realizing that these children have come here as our teachers and that we still all have a lot to learn. I spent a lot of time during the life of my Star child in esoteric bookstores and attending classes to learn more about what he experienced "naturally".

In all the cases above, there is one overriding quality which will serve us well and that is **to be present.** So many times, we have all seen busy, distracted parents dragging their children through the streets and stores. The child is talking, but no one is listening. The child often starts to yell or scream at the parent.

Today, I heard a little boy yelling in the bakery. His mother told him to be quiet. This continued and she took him out of the bakery and into the street where he really became angry. She still continued to shout at him and he became more and more upset. Finally, at her wit's end, she stopped, became present, and asked him what was wrong. He became quiet and explained what he wanted. **End of story and a lesson for the mother in being present.**

So many of our problems in general can be easily solved if we stay present in the moment. After all, fear enters the scene usually only when we are thinking of the future. It is interesting how we can find simple solutions to what appear to be overwhelming problems and situations when we take a few moments to breathe and become present. We can just take in three breaths of peace and exhale three times thinking of becoming calm. This simple exercise will help us to be present in our own lives and with our children. We can also teach this to our children, even when they are very young.

Exercise for children (calming and being present)

Stand in front of your child and make eye contact. Then, just say these simple words while breathing in deeply: *"Breathing in, I am happy."* And on the out breathe, you say, *"Breathing out, I smile."* Ask your child to join you in slowly breathing in and out. You can also say the words together, which makes the exercise more powerful and helps create an intimate joining. Such a simple exercise – yet it can work wonders.

Chapter Two:

Listening is Loving

Listening to our children is part of being present. We have already seen the importance of being present in the here and now. When our children experience something differently than what is considered "normal", we need to be as fully present as possible. When they tell us about their dreams, their encounters with spirit beings, and especially when they tell us about their star of origin, we really must listen to them.

When I am listening to a Star child, I attempt to enter as fully as possible into her world. This seems to be the most beneficial way of interacting with a child in situation that can seem very foreign to you. Sometimes, because I am very visual and easily distracted, I close my eyes and attempt to experience what the child is telling me. If you are going to use this method, be sure to tell the child what you are doing. *"I'm going to close my eyes while you talk so that I can try to see what you have or are experiencing"*. You have to know yourself and the child you are with well enough to know if this is an effective method to use.

What are the techniques that can enhance listening?

The first thing that I would advise is to listen without interrupting. For example, let us say that your child enters the house because he has just "seen" a fairy in the garden. He may be very excited, frightened, agitated, or completely matter of fact about it. When he begins to tell you about what he has seen, it is best to stop what you are doing immediately, to make eye contact with him, and to listen carefully to the details. Of course, you will have a million questions, but save those for later. First, allow the child to tell the story all the way through. Sometimes, children will need to repeat it two or three times before they feel heard.

No matter how strange the story may seem, attempt to accept it as true and real for your child. She will be able to detect your skepticism and your doubts if you have them (more about this in a moment). *Remember, I said accept it as true and real for your child.*

This means that whatever the child is talking about doesn't have to be real for you. This is a point to remember because it will make acceptance of your child's world easier for you.

Another example, let us say that your child comes running in from the outdoors, shouting that she had been killed when she was a little Chinese girl. The first thing to do is breathe and attempt to relax. Second, do not negate what she is telling you. Now, remember to make eye contact and don't try to figure anything out at this point. Make eye contact and allow her to tell you the story, whatever it may be.

Of course, as adults we are wondering what could have caused this experience – too much television, etc. and while we are listening we are often looking for a reason to explain what the child is telling us. Attempt to let go of all your preconceived ideas and just listen. *Turn off your logical mind as much as possible and try to enter into your child's world and experience.* Don't worry if you don't do it "right" the first few times. All of these techniques take time and patience for you to learn.

Once the story is clear and the child seems satisfied, the next step is to affirm what she has just shared. Part of good listening is to acknowledge that what the person has just shared is true for them. So some statements to that effect are in order. For example, you might say, *"You sound really excited about having seen that fairy."* or *"You seem really happy to have heard the angel speak to you."* or *"That must have been fun (or whatever your child's state is – difficult, scary) for you."* In this way, your child will feel that you have not only heard her, but that you also understand how she feels. It is probably good to hold your own thoughts of how you might feel in a similar situation and not share those just yet.

Then you can begin to ask questions. The questions should always be those, which indicate that you believe your child or at least that you are interested in what she is telling you. They should also be questions which are called "opened ended" ones. Let me explain. If you ask your child a "closed ended" question, it evokes very little response. An example: "Did you see the Angel here?" Answer: "Yes." or "No". So a question, which can potentially be responded to with a "yes" or "no" is closed ended because it does not encourage further conversation.

So what kinds of questions are appropriate and "open ended"? One good question to begin with starts with the word "where"? *"Where did you see the fairy?"* or *"Where did you have this experience?"* Then go out in the garden with your child and listen to what he says. You can now ask for more details, sometimes asking "closed ended" questions: *"What did the fairy look like?" "Was it like the one in your little fairy book?" "Have you seen fairies before?" "What do you think the little fairy was doing there?"* and so on. Here you are attempting to understand your child's experience and at the same time see if you really believe that the child experienced something.

I once met the charming Star child granddaughter of a friend of mine in Canada who very definitely had the ability to see and to talk to plant fairies or spirits. One day in my friend's garden, the little girl pointed them out to me and engaged in a very real conversation with them. She explained why one plant had more fairies around it than the others; and she did so in a very serious manner. When she suddenly saw one, she was thrilled with a big smile all over her face; and when she couldn't see them she was visibly sad.

I don't believe she was making them up, even though at the time, I couldn't see them. Once she realized that her granddaughter could see them, her grandmother had purchased a book of flower fairies for her. The child said that the pictures "weren't real" – that the fairies didn't look at all like the silly fairies in the book. It seems to me if she were making it all up and wanted her grandmother to believe her, she would have happily wanted us to believe that she had seen the fairies just like the "real" ones in the book!

So many times parents decide that their children have vivid imaginations and then negate their experiences. This can be very destructive for the child and for your relationship with your child. Star children often have the ability to see spirits, to see auras, to hear voices, to move things through the air, and to remember past lives and other dimensions, and so do a lot of children. In order to find out more about their beliefs and their worlds, we must listen.

Now what about the little girl who believed she was killed when she was Chinese in another life? What if she were your child? How would you handle this? I had a similar experience with my son when he was about four-years-old and I must say that it was a very upsetting experience for me and for him. Remember, no matter how agitated your child is, stop, breathe, make eye contact, and listen.

Star children often have what I call "spontaneous past life recall". This recall can occur at any time and may or may not be triggered by a preceding event. By this I mean, sometimes a child's past life recall will be triggered by something he has seen or heard – a television program, a book he has read or a place he visits. And at other times, these recalls just seem to occur without any apparent rime or reason.

The child may be eating, playing, studying, and suddenly will say something to indicate she remembers a past life. In the case of my son, he actually saw his past lives like a film passing before his eyes and then experienced some of the pain associated with his previous deaths.

Typical statements, which may startle parents are ones like these: A three year old girl says to her mother while eating, "I remember when I was the Mommy and you were my little girl". Or "I remember when Johnnie (now the child's brother) was my Daddy". Or "Do you remember the day it snowed and we were all killed in the car?" Or a child might say to his pregnant mother, "I don't want you to have the same sister that I had last time". Or "Why is Grandmother wanting to come back so soon? Isn't she happy where she is?"

Star children frequently remember not only past lives, but lives in between lives! They also seem to be able to talk to people who are dead and exist in the other dimensions, and they can often predict deaths. For instance, there are many documented cases of children waking up in the morning and asking their parents why "Grandpa was flying by and saying goodbye" or why "Grandma was crying and saying she couldn't play anymore." Of course, shortly thereafter word is received that the grandparent had died.

So, we must listen carefully and with full attention. We must never negate the child's reality, even if it proves to be erroneous. However, of course, as in the case of predicting a death, we must comfort our child and explain that while what he has dreamt or seen may be very real and come to pass, we hope along with him that it is not true. We can then also explain later on in the day, if it is not true, why we might dream such things.

For instance, we can explain that fears we have during the day might cause us to have these kinds of dreams at night. Dreams serve us by helping us understand our unresolved emotions and fears.

One of the most touching stories that I have read was about a little boy and his teacher/dolphin named Bee. After spending many hours in the water swimming with Bee who would patiently hold up cards with words on them, the little boy, who had delayed speech problems, learned to speak and communicate. One night, he woke up crying inconsolably. He was crying out, "My Bee. Oh, my poor Bee." The next morning, his parents were told that Bee had died during the night. I find this story extraordinarily touching.

Star children may live in extremely unusual worlds and have perceptions that are way beyond the ordinary. One woman relates how as she walked through the city streets at about the age of five or six she would 'see' countless people – some with feet suspended in the air as if using a pavement higher than the one that was presently visible.

Nobody else could see these figures and when she realized that fact, she blocked them out and says, "I just stopped seeing them"[1].

When we are present and really listening to our children, we can enter more and more into their worlds. The more open and accepting you are able to be, the more your child can open, trust and share with you. We are not here to judge our children or each other for that matter, but to learn to be more loving each day. There is so much more to our "world" than we actually are able to perceive. I believe that by helping our children be unlimited, we also expand our own consciousness.

We need to foster the belief in the reality of our unlimited potential as human beings, because the information necessary to heal our planet will come from unseen sources, in dreams, from guides and other entities. New healing paradigms and ways to clean up the environment will be brought in through Star children, and these children know that. They know their purpose and their mission.

Once, I was working with a mother and her two small children. The little boy, age three, always wanted to touch his baby brother's head. And the mother thought that he was trying to hurt his brother. I asked the little boy, who obviously had great healing ability, to come and put his hands on his brother's head. When he did so, the baby stopped crying. The little Star child worked very seriously and for a long time. Afterwards, he told his mother that he was just trying to fix his brother's head because it had been "dented when he was born."

Many Star children have healing abilities themselves and others are able to channel information through and bring new healing modalities to Earth. I have already had the pleasure and honor of contact with a very charming being that channeled through a whole new healing system called the Enelph Method. It is being practiced in France with good results. I am one among many who are accessing these higher energies for the betterment of human beings everywhere. So we have very good reasons to value and encourage our children's insights!

There is a significant difference between the child who is listened to and whose beliefs and experiences are affirmed by those around and the child whose parents are closed to such events. The child that is affirmed learns gradually that not all children can perceive things as he/she can and accepts their differences without problems. Honoring the beliefs of Star children, and for that matter of everyone, is an essential step in peacemaking. The child who is ridiculed, laughed at or told to stop having such experiences, or to stop telling lies goes "underground". That is, their belief systems and psychic abilities become hidden from the world and that part is often inaccessible even to the child himself.

This creates a very unhealthy atmosphere for the child to live in. It is as if a very large part of the child's world is not acceptable, is weird and thus shame may enter the picture. It often takes a lifetime to reintegrate this part. I can speak for myself and say that I spent many years feeling as if I were crazy, only to find out that I am more sensitive than most people and that I have obvious psychic abilities. The first part of my life was spent trying to "not see what other people didn't see" which was the advice that my psychic father gave me when I was eight-years-old.

I remember the event quite clearly. My parents were able to tolerate such things as my talking to myself, my horrendous nightmares and the time I "became a bird and spent hours being the bird in the tree". They also were able to accept when I would privately tell them things which were going to happen or had already happened that I had no way of knowing. Fortunately, my clairvoyant flashes were infrequent when I was a child. My parents knew I was different, though it was never outwardly acknowledged. Years later at a family gathering, I learned that my cousins thought I was "weird" and that some of them were even afraid of me because of my abilities.

My patient older brother also was challenged by my presence, though luckily he loves me dearly and accepts me as his bright, eccentric sister. He had to tolerate years of being called, "Jew Jew", as that was my loving nickname for him. Was this something left over from my past life where I was killed in a concentration camp? And is it just a coincidence that I was brought into the world by a dear old German doctor? Perhaps, the karma from that life has been burned off.

Here is a rather memorable example of my being clairvoyant. Once when I was about eight-years-old, my aunt and uncle arrived back at their house where I had been staying with my older brother. They had some very sad news to tell us. I said that I already knew my little brother had died and that we did not want to talk about it. I clearly remember then going into the bedroom and playing checkers with my older brother. No one ever asked me how I knew. In fact, I had "seen" the whole thing as it happened. Though I can't remember exactly how I had "seen" this, I'm sure that I probably had a dream or vision of him being taken away by the angels. Didn't everyone? At that time, I just assumed my older brother had been able to "see" the same as I had and that he already knew as well.

Just last week, I was walking in the park with a good friend of mine when I announced that his mother was going to die soon. Later in the week, I had three dreams about death and the Angel of Death. His mother is in critical condition in the hospital as I am writing this.

In any case, my family was pretty typical of many families. As long as the "secret" remained within the safe family limits, my odd behavior was acceptable. However, there is one day I remember when I crossed over the acceptable limits. My father's sister came to dinner and at the table, I went over and hugged her and told her I felt sad, too, that her dog had died. All hell broke loose at the table. My aunt started to cry, my father started to shout at me, my mother sent me to my room and there I sat, stunned and unclear about what had just happened.

My father came into my bedroom with a very stern look on his face. He sat down next to me and said, "Don't ever talk about the things that you "know" that other people don't know about. Also, don't ever talk about things that you "know" if the other person hasn't already talked about it." He then walked out, leaving me at eight years of age in a very confused state.

How could I know what other people knew? How could I know what I knew that other people didn't know? How could I be sure that they had already talked about it out loud when sometimes I could hear people talk and their lips didn't move? Shortly after this episode I had to start wearing glasses to see far away. It is quite unbelievable to think that there was such a direct correlation between this confusing event and my diminished eyesight.

From then on, I tried to be a good daughter. In fact, recently my mother told me I was a very easy child to raise. Had she forgotten the time she took me to the doctor to report on my strange behavior? I remember looking through the door as she was telling the doctor about my predictions and nightmares. To this day, I don't know if the door was really open or not. The doctor said that I was like a finely tuned violin and that I must be protected or else I might break. Now that was a scary thought! How might I break?

I tell you all this from my personal experience just to emphasize how important it is to listen to your children. It is never easy to be different even if you have what some people would consider to be gifts or talents. A child likes to be accepted by his peers, well, don't we all?

I remember being very sad one day when I came home from school because some children would not play with me. My mother made it very clear when I was quite young that not everyone would like me. She explained that it was just a simple fact of life, that certain people like each other and others do not, so I have never been especially surprised when someone doesn't like me. She emphasized that it was more important to be oneself; after all we could never make everyone like us no matter how hard we try. She said I would be happiest if I were myself because then I would be true to myself. And this information has helped me a lot and I think it is something valuable to pass on to our children and to each other.

Although I am giving you a lot of information and advice about how to listen to your children, how to be honest, loving, and accepting, I also know there are days where we are all less than perfect. Surely, my parents did not do everything right and neither did I with my son. We all have moments where life seems too difficult to carry on, when we don't have one more ounce of patience, when we want our children and the whole world to disappear. This is perfectly natural and human. All the practical tips in this second part of the book are given to help you be better parents, not to make you feel like you will never "measure up"!

So, let's go over the skills that can help us be better listeners, not only with children, but also with everyone that is important to us.

1. First, take a few deep breaths, just to become more present in the moment.
2. Make eye contact and begin to listen to what is being said.
3. Give signs that you are listening by nodding your head, facial expressions, and little affirmative words, such as, "Hum", "Ah ha", etc.
4. Allow the person to repeat the story as many times as necessary, without interrupting or judging him. From time to time, you may give feedback to verify that your perceptions are correct.
5. Acknowledge what they have experienced and what they are feeling.
6. Ask "open ended" questions and then you may include some "closed ended" questions, especially if the child is quite young, to get more detail.
7. Bring the experience to closure by summing up the experience and specifically keeping the door open to more sharing about these sorts of adventures. You might say something like this, *"Gee, this has been quite an exciting day. Whenever you have a similar experience, be sure and tell me because it's very interesting."* For a younger child, you might say, *"Mommy (Daddy) loves to hear your stories. Be sure to keep telling them to me."*

Also, I would advise you to keep a journal of the unusual things that your Star child experiences or relates to you. Later on this can prove invaluable, especially if the child starts to forget or denies that he ever had psychic abilities, past life recall or memories of his or her star.

Some children become bound by the Earth's dense vibrations and forget their past lives or where they have come from. One young woman who, as a child, recalled her life on another star, recently told me that she did not believe in all that "New Age" stuff anymore. She has, in fact, joined the Communist party. Ah, growing up and growing wise is never easy to do.

We can use these listening skills no matter what our child is sharing, whether he is trying to find a solution to a problem, telling us about something she or he is about to do or asking for our advice. *Listening is love made manifest.* We can help our Star children and everyone around us find their own best answers when we listen to them. We can point to possible directions, open doors for them but we cannot lead their lives, for the lives of our children belong to the future, a portal we cannot cross.

Chapter Three:
Trust You Must

Trusting our children's intuition and guidance can often be very challenging, especially in the case of Star children. Many of them have the habit of just "knowing" things and saying things as if everyone else does too. Remember they already know why they are here and what their mission is. Let us first examine how these Star children access their knowledge.

I have already mentioned that many Star children have built in knowledge of another way of being or living, which seems to come from an ancient memory from life on another planet. There are many theories about this. Some people believe these memories may be embedded in the DNA itself; others, believe that these children may be part of an "alien conspiracy"; some believe that these children are messengers from other planets. There are several books on the market that you can read in additional to those I have referenced.

While my son believed that he was from another planet or star, I never thought of him as an "alien", nor did I ever think that I had been abducted and impregnated by an extraterrestrial. However, I do not deny that these things may be taking place and that others believe or have actually experienced such things.

Marcus simply stated that he was from another star and that he remembered his star. This was done in a very matter of fact way, as is the case with most Star children. They may have a tendency to love stargazing and all things to do with the cosmos. Most of them, however, do not talk about, nor remember much about other life forms, or, if they do, it simply doesn't seem important to their mission.

When a Star child talks about his or her home planet, you may notice that the whole atmosphere around the child changes. Everything becomes quiet and there may even be a light or a sense of the sacred at that moment. When you listen to a Star child tell about his or her home planet, there is no question in your mind that the child is telling you something, which is completely true for him. There is a certain discernable look in the eyes – often the child looks up into the space of memory access. We usually look upward to access stored informational data or to recall things from our past experiences.

There is also a yearning to go back to their star. This can be perceived in their bodies, in their faces and especially in their eyes. Once you have this experience with a Star child, there is no doubt ever again in your mind that there are children and adults here from other stars. Interestingly, each child has the same atmosphere, the same longing and the same look.

How this memory is accessed is difficult to discern. The memory I have of my star, a place of love and light, comes to me during quiet times and in my dreams. Is this really a star, another planet or merely a memory of the Universal Spirit? I am not sure. What I am convinced of is that the memory seems real to those of us who have it. Many Star children become teary eyed the moment I start to speak about other stars and vibrations.

Recently, at a Conference for the New Children in Holland, I gave a lecture about Star children. Some people had tears in their eyes, and when I asked how many people believed they were from other stars, at least one-third put up their hands. Can we all be wrong? Can we all be a part of mass hypnosis? I think not; the longing to return home is too real. By the way, people often cry when I speak in public, as if there is some energy coming through me that triggers ancient memories of another way of being.

So there is this belief that Star children have that they have come from another star or vibration. There is also a yearning to go back to that place and a feeling that they do not want to be here on Earth or that they do not fit it. We, as parents, must trust the Divine Plan as is being revealed through our children. At the same time, we must assume our roles as guides for them on Planet Earth.

Many Star children are in constant or sporadic contact with their guides or angels. My son was convinced that he had guides who had prepared him for the life he lived before he was born and who accompanied him throughout his Earth journey. Many children and adults feel the same way. Remember you may be a Star child and be a parent or even a grandparent to one.

We have to trust our children in their "knowing" and in their guidance. Many of them take on huge tasks before we think they are ready to do so. For instance, I know of children starting university at fifteen-years-old, running their own businesses at twelve, and undertaking large social reform actions while still adolescents. I have known young children who decide to be actors, they phone agents and land parts; and those who apply to universities and leave high school for early admission without consulting their parents! They just "know" what is right for them.

I have had Star children in sessions ask me to whom they should listen, their parents or their guides? This is always a hard question to answer because I normally trust that both guides and parents have good advice for their children. In this case, I listen carefully to the situation and then to the advice given by both. I attempt to merge the advice or directives of both the parent and the guide. Frequently, the child, like most human beings, is caught in black or white thinking, where one person must be right and the other wrong. Very often, the guidance I give is enough to help the child see that the parent and the guide are working together to lead or point her in the right direction or to make the best decision.

How are Star children in contact with their guides? They often hear a voice "in their heads" which tells them the best thing to do in any given situation. Some children may silently call out or evoke their guides when they are in a particularly trying situation. Some "see" their guides as "imaginary friends", spirits, angels, or in human form, in which case they can carry on normal conversations with them. Some report that their guides come in their dreams or when they are bored in class. Others channel their guides through automatic writing, inner listening or inner dictation. Some believe that their guides give them signs in the real world – like words which are on license plates, green or red traffic signal lights, passages in books, or even words of people who are in conversation with others. And some say, they don't know how they "know" things, they just do.

This brings up the subject of imaginary friends. Are they guides, angels, or spirits who have passed on? One author explains, "The imaginary friend experienced by many children has exasperated many parents and teachers. The phenomenon has a variety of possible explanations: The child could be communicating with the spirit of an animal or dead child, or with a fairy, angel, sprite or extraterrestrial. She or he could be having a telepathic or out-of-body experience, or it could simply be the child's vivid imagination. I have, however, read accounts of people other than the child being able to see the imaginary friend. Sometimes children discover imaginary friends when they are lonely or sick – having someone always around can be very comforting.

Some children talk to their friend in a language no one else understands. There is no reason for alarm on the part of the parent, unless the imaginary friend tells the child to do evil or destructive things. In that case professional assistance would certainly be desirable. Again, patience is the key word. Ridiculing or denying the existence of the imaginary friend or mocking the child in any way can do irreparable damage, causing the child to suppress his or her emotions and feel it is unsafe to confide in the parent. It is not necessary to make a big issue of this; the parent can simply ask about the friend, accept it as natural, and usually the child will simply grow out of it"[2].

Yes, it is true and all too sad that many children do "outgrow" their imaginary friends who may actually be their spirit guides or angels. Personally, I would encourage a child to continue speaking to his or her imaginary friend, especially if he or she provides good guidance for your child.

Perhaps here is a good place to explain the different types of knowing that we may have as human beings. These ways of knowing may be called "psychic" or simply "other ways". In other words, we are talking here of ways of "knowing" something which is beyond the intellect and beyond ordinary explication.

Clairvoyance means literally "to see clearly" when translated directly from the French. It is the ability to see beyond the normal range of visions – to "see" events that are taking place in the present generally at another location. This may also be called "remote viewing" meaning just that – the ability to view an event that takes place outside of normal vision.

An example, once when I was asleep in Pittsburgh, Pennsylvania, I "saw" a man look into the bathroom window of my sister's home who was then living in California. I woke up with a fright. The next day when I called her in California, I found out that she had gotten up in the middle of the night to use the bathroom and she had seen a man looking in the bathroom window.

Clairaudience is the ability to hear words or voices inside your head, as if someone is actually speaking to you. "Channeling" can be a type of clairaudience; a person hears words like an inner dictation and either repeats them or writes them out. There is another type of channeling in which the person moves aside his personality and individuality and allows another entity to enter his energy field or body and speak through him.

An example: A man was about to get on an airplane, when he heard a voice in his head that told him not to go on that plane. Later in the day, he hears that that flight had mechanical trouble and while it landed safely, some of the passengers were injured.

Clairsentience is the ability to psychically feel information or impressions. This can be a bodily sensation like "a gut reaction" or "a feeling, intuition or knowing" about something or someone.

An example: At one time I dated a very nice, handsome, seemingly kind man that had a lovely penthouse apartment. The first time I used the bathroom in his bedroom, I had a very uneasy, even frightening feeling all over my body – a feeling that I needed to get out of his apartment fast. Luckily, I was never intimate with him. The next woman he was with ended up hospitalized, near death, as he had beaten her up in his bedroom. Needless to say, I was very grateful to be clairsentient.

Precognition is from the Latin meaning "to know before", which is the ability to know the future and/or to make predictions of future happenings. Precognition may come through a vision, a dream, a feeling, or simply a knowing.

We all have many, many examples of this. You suddenly think about someone and there they are in front of you. You have a feeling of dread throughout the day, and then you receive bad news. You see yourself living in a certain house, and then you find it. You have a feeling to check your tires before you drive your car and, sure enough, there is a problem.

Psychic Empathy is the capacity to merge with someone else and experience the world as they do. According to Dr. Judith Orloff, psychic empaths can "feel what's going on inside others both emotionally and physically as if it were happening to them"[3]. Some empaths are unable to distinguish the sensations of others from their own.

As an example, a friend of mine, who is a psychic empath was recently on a train resting comfortably when suddenly she felt increasingly nervous and irritated. This continued for a few moments and soon she felt a lot of pressure in her head as if it were about to blow up. Just when she was trying to figure out if these feelings were hers or not, the man behind her stood up and started shouting. He was extremely angry and continued to shout on and off for a period of time. When she realized that she had been "picking up" his anger and tension in his body, she could go back to peacefully reading her book.

Some Star children may be so sensitive that they are unable to go to school or even in extreme cases leave their homes, though for most children this sensitivity poses no problem. Dr. Orloff believes that "many agoraphobics are terrified of leaving their homes because they're actually undiagnosed psychic empaths"[4]. If your child has this heightened sensitivity, there are therapists, psychics and healers who can teach him or her how to handle these feelings. It is best if the helping professionals, themselves, have experience in this area.

Of course, we have all had the experience of being with someone who is feeling down or extremely elated and afterwards we feel the same way. And who hasn't had the experience of a funny feeling somewhere in his or her body, only to have someone close complaint of a pain in the same spot? If your child has a frequent physical complaint, check to see if he or she is not picking up a symptom, which belongs to someone else. An empathic child who sits next to another child with a physical aliment may also experience the same discomfort.

Telekinesis is the ability to move objects with the mind.

Uri Geller, a well-known Israeli psychic, is very gifted in this area. Most of us have witnessed his demonstrations on television of bending metal with his mind, or we have read about them. While some think that he uses a form of magic and psychic abilities, there have been studies conducted, which prove otherwise.

I have a friend who has many bent spoons hidden away in a drawer. They are a memory of an experiment in which she learned how to bend spoons. My son also had the ability to move objects with his mind and I remember when I was very small, I used to sit and call an object to my hand. While I never succeeded, at least I remembered that I once was able to do it in another lifetime.

This is a story I love to tell about my own Star child. One evening his father went upstairs to tuck Marcus in and saw that he had many toys on the floor and all over his bed. While the toys on the floor were nothing unusual, his father noticed the ones on his bed seemed to be carefully placed, as if someone else had put them there after he had crawled into bed. He asked Marcus what had happened and he replied, "I have been moving things around. I just think about my toys coming off the shelf to my bed and they do. This way I don't have to get out of bed to get them." Quite a useful skill, don't you think?

Telepathy is the ability to communicate directly from mind to mind without the use of words.

An example: You are home one night and feeling alone. Suddenly, you wish a certain person would call you. He does. Very often parents have a strong telepathic connection with their children. Have you ever been troubled and had your parent call? I have traveled miles to turn up at someone's doorstep just when they needed me. We have all had these types of experiences. We can often hear each other's thoughts and hear each other's call for help.

Actually, I believe everyone has psychic abilities; it is just that a lot of people have forgotten about them. It is interesting in my sessions with people that many will initially say that they are not psychic and do not even believe in it. Later in the session, when I ask questions about their ability to "know" something, they will often launch into a story filled with psychic experiences. When I make them conscious of their perceptions, they are surprised and very often pleased.

It is interesting to note that some Star children do not carry over their psychic abilities from one lifetime to the next. My son, who has now reincarnated, was very psychic. Now, in his new body, he has just begun to see auras again at age seventeen. Sometimes this can be frustrating, but I'm convinced that our gifts and talents often remain "hidden" for good reasons.

Star children have an intuitive quality that works very well for them. They very often demonstrate a remarkable insight into the character of others. It is interesting to note that a Star child may take a sudden dislike to someone without any apparent reason, only to find out later that the person has a dark side or a mean streak. Also, the Star child may have the most unusual friends, sometimes children much older than they are or those with completely different interests. They can be easily repelled or attracted to someone, and we must learn to trust their intuitions and their "unusual" abilities.

I believe that Star children have this psychic sense as a sort of inner guidance that helps them achieve their life goals and mission. Sometimes, they have a past life memory which causes them to need to be in someone's company for a period of time. Other times, they have met a kindred soul or another Star child. They may need to receive information or give a message to the person, and at other times, the affinity is inexplicable.

When we learn to trust ourselves with our children and we learn to trust our children's knowingness, we teach our children to trust more in themselves and their abilities. This trust in them can help them immensely, as it can be difficult to be different in the world of their peers. If they know that they are accepted and loved by their parents and that they honored and treasured their abilities, Star children will surely grow up to be the peacemakers that they are meant to be. They will grow up proud with a sense that they have something valuable and important to contribute to the society in which they live. Through them and their ways of remembering, their ability to create, to think in innovative ways, to invent technology, to improve and clean up the environment, we shall all benefit.

Chapter Four:
Stand Guard

Star children, even though they can be very independent and possess a knowing beyond their Earth years, often need to be protected from what I call "incompatible vibrations". There is a delicate line between protecting them and allowing them to experience life on Earth. If you have a Star child or if you are one, you will understand these last two statements immediately. But if you are not, I will go into a bit more detail here. Also remember that many Star children are perfectly able to protect themselves.

What are "incompatible vibrations"? This is anything and anyone who disturbs your child beginning when he or she is a baby. If florescent lights irritate your child, certain kinds of music, violent television shows or movies, or various foods, these intrusions should be kept to a minimum as much as possible. I have seen children who simply could not attend school because of the lighting or the noise or even the other children.

Many Star children are able to attend school sporadically with a plethora of illnesses filling in the time at home. I believe that the stimuli of school is simply too much for these very sensitive children, just as the atmosphere of large cities can be too strong energetically for adult Star children. Illnesses often consist of feelings of weakness, tiredness, inexplicable fatigue and so on. The solution is usually withdrawal, some quiet reading, listening to music, or resting during which time they are recharging their batteries and getting fortified for the next foray out into the "real world". For many of them, I suspect these "time-outs" are an opportunity to come back to themselves and a time to tune into their greater mission, though I have no hard proof of this.

I have heard of many Star children that use this time out to create art projects, write stories or work on computer projects. It is as if their souls or inner knowing guide them to express what needs to be expressed. I have asked a few of them why they can't go to school and the usual response is that they are simply too tired, "no energy". They often want to go, but just can't.

Because they are usually very bright children, their schoolwork doesn't seem to suffer. Some parents also opt for home schooling in those countries where it is legal. My son attended a small country day school where he thrived because everyone seemed to accept each child's individual differences.

When considering alternative schooling, you as parents should consider values education as an important selection criteria. The Brahma Kumaris World Spiritual University describes these universally recognized values as cooperation, freedom, happiness, honesty, humility, love, peace, respect, responsibility, simplicity, tolerance, and unity. "Such higher order values transcend the uniqueness of humanity's richly diverse cultural, philosophical, and social heritage, forming a common bedrock on which to build not only friendly international relations but also mutual benefit in one-on-one interactions. . .They will touch the core of the individual, perhaps inspiring positive change which can contribute to world transformation. The world will automatically become a better place when each individual becomes a better person"[5].

Values are very necessary and I encourage you to read publications by this wonderful organization, the Brahma Kumaris, whose activities are "grounded in the belief that the world needs to invest more resources in education of its peoples with sound human, moral and spiritual values"[6].

Star children also need to be protected from others who simply do not understand them. Sometimes, helpful relatives or friends may imply that your child should be in school or should be able to do a certain activity like all children his or her age, since there is apparently nothing really wrong with her or him. I have seen parents challenged by all kinds of well meaning people including school authorities and medical doctors. You need to be the judge of what your child can handle. There are many fine solutions. Sometimes, just a change of school or curriculum can make all the difference in the world.

I remember one student who was barely passing his subjects at school. He had to study too long in the evenings, leaving no time for day dreaming, creating and studying music. He was studying four languages, which is not unusual in Europe. I suggested that he drop Latin or

Greek and this was just what he needed in order to get through the school year. He barely squeaked through on the national exams, but now he is at a university and once again at the top of his class. What made the difference? Part of it was just lightening the scholastic load and the other was moving out of the family home. Remember these children pick up a lot of the thoughts and feelings of the people around them.

Watching who interacts with your child and how they do so is also necessary. Those who do not understand your child should be encouraged to have as little interaction as possible. Normally, this will be self-regulated by your Star child, as dislikes and likes can be rather strong and clearly defined. This means that if your child does not like your mother/father/sister/brother, he or she will let you know and even refuse to be in the same room as they are. This can make for rather unusual holiday celebrations; yet if you know what to expect, your level of anxiety and tension can be diminished. It is of course important to point out to your child what is socially acceptable behavior.

Often, the child will agree to participate in a family gathering if he or she can just stay close to you or another family member. Remember that giving your child a choice, for instance as to where to sit at the table, can work wonders. Whether or not you force your child to participate in a family gathering is always your judgment call. Star children cooperate best when their ideas and feelings are honored and when they have some say in the matter before them. Talking things through always helps because Star children are usually reasonable human beings.

Star children have come here to experience Earth life. They are not meant to be a burden. While they are very wise beings, they can have difficulties interacting with children of their own age. Here is where your guidance can help. Also, at an early age you can easily teach them how to protect themselves against these negative energies. They learn quickly, almost as if they are recalling something that was known once, but now forgotten. Many of the very young Star children are being born with the ability to handle all sorts of Earth energies and will not need to learn how to protect themselves.

How can we help our children protect themselves against incompatible vibrations?

Here are some simple exercises which can be taught quickly and which work well.

If your child is super sensitive, she or he needs insulation from the world. While standing in front of your child, say the following:

(For a child up to eight-years-old or so.) *Close your eyes and imagine that there's a big flashlight above you that is shining its light all around you. This is a special, magical light because nothing can enter into the light unless you want it to. So, the next time (here you give the situation, for example, the next time you are at school and feel sort of strange in the hall) just remember to turn on the big flashlight and have it shine on you. Whatever is bothering you, will just run away from the light.*

For an older child: *Close your eyes and imagine that there is a beam of golden light (or any other bright color – perhaps your child's favorite one) which is falling over you, much like a fountain of water. The light feels warm and you feel very relaxed in it. This is a healing light that will protect you from whatever is disturbing to you. Anytime you feel upset, frustrated or out of balance in any way, you can just call to this beam of light and it will appear. The light creates a shield that won't allow anything negative to enter.*

You may have to repeat the exercise a few times with your child. I would have some "dress rehearsals" with him or her, much as we do during a fire drill. You explain that from time to time in the next few days, you are going to practice with them so that when they really need to protect themselves it will be almost automatic. You can use the good example of a fire drill if you are in a country where the children practice such things in school. If not, you can use another example – perhaps you live in earthquake country or in a severe weather area.

You explain how you are prepared in advance for events that may occur in order to keep people from panicking. When you know what to do and how to do it, you can feel relaxed, knowing that if the storm (or whatever) should arrive you have a plan to reach a safe area. These can serve as examples. By the way, it is always a good idea to practice with your children how they would get out of the house in the event of a fire!

Okay, back to practice. You explain that as sort of a game, over the next few days, and they'll never know when, you are going to say *"flashlight"* or *"shield"* and they are to throw up their beam of light. For the little ones, this can really be a game, yet you are giving them a valuable tool to use. Once they know how to shield themselves, out they go into the world to practice. It might be wise, especially if you have a child with serious fears, to accompany them for a trial run. So if they have trouble operating in malls for example, you go there with them at a time when it is moderately busy. Remember that we want them to succeed, so do not put them in a very difficult situation like Saturday afternoon at the mall.

Once they succeed, they will have more and more confidence in confronting the problem. Each time, they learn how to protect themselves and cope in the world; they are one step closer to realizing their peace mission.

Star children often feel different from their peers and they can feel sad about this. Many of them are out and out rejected by other children at school because of their differences. Some just have a difficult time with their peers because they don't understand "normal" Earth behavior. It is difficult for them to understand ideas of competition and behavior, which are not loving. Many Star children socialize better with adults than other children, though all thrive when they meet other Star children.

We must protect them from feeling that their differences are burdens. Some of them are frightened when they find out that not everyone believes what they believe. Be sure to keep the lines of communication open. And if you do not know what they are talking about or feeling, find someone who does. A good place to start is with the Internet. Sometimes, all you need is to connect with another parent who has a Star child and at other times you have to actually find a professionally trained person to help.

We may have to help our children trust in their abilities, to know and to see their differences as gifts, and not as burdens. This depends a lot on how you view your child. The children who fare the best are those who are loved and valued by their parents. When parents honor their children's differences, the child learns to do the same. There are many good books and resources on the market that you can use as reference.

Occasionally, a Star child will be disturbed if in the beginning she or he only "picks up" on a psychic level those events which are sad or negative, like the death of someone close. This is a common phenomenon with unskilled psychics. With a little encouragement and practice your child can learn to open his or her awareness to the whole fascinating world of psychic phenomena.

Finally, we need to trust that our Star child, with his or her particular destiny, arrived at our doorstep not by accident, but through some Divine Plan. Many Star children report that they have chosen their parents before they were born. Some report "seeing and choosing" their parents while they were still in the sky. If this is true, then we can surely trust that we have the abilities to accommodate our child and his or her differences, along with his or her magnificent gifts. A Star child is a miracle, a challenge, a gift, a door opener, a peacemaker, and a teacher – all at once.

Chapter Five:

In Secure Hands: Heart to Heart

Star children need to know that they have caring, loving parents who understand them. They also need parents who remain in their ultimate roles as parents who are on Earth to guide, teach and love their children. This means that even when you are confronted with a child who apparently "knows" more than you, you are still the one setting up the guidelines for them and their behavior. In all of nature, of which we are a part, parents take care of their young until they are ready to go out on their own. Animals basically teach their young how to survive in their environment and we must do the same, especially with Star children. These children may come to this world with a great deal of spiritual knowledge, but with very few coping skills to function here.

Most Star children are easy going spirits who want to please others, and still, they have very definite ideas. As one teacher says, "Parents do not help their children by explaining that they are 'Indigo Children' and then allowing them to misbehave without boundaries and guidelines. Even children who could eventually raise the consciousness of the planet need boundaries. With boundaries, self-control is learned, which is integral for a peaceful community"[7]. I believe we need to honor Star children and their beliefs, while simultaneously helping them to understand that the world operates within limits, at least as of today!

I have already mentioned earlier one tool that is good to keep in mind. That is, something may be perfect for your Star child in keeping with his or her beliefs, but does not necessarily have to be accepted by everyone. An example: Marcus, my son, believed that he was from another star, which he talked about to me. However, to my knowledge he never spoke about this to people who would not be able to understand. At an early age, in fact, he explained to me that everyone around us was in a certain "grade" in Earth school. We simply had to know that and realize that those in the lower grades would not be ready for the advanced stuff.

If your Star child insists on telling your parents about his or her beliefs for instance, you must explain to your child about the different grade levels if you think they are likely to ridicule him or her. It is, however, amazing the things that grandparents will accept and try to understand when their grandchildren speak. For some of you, it is interesting to remember that they, as parents, had no patience at all with your fantasies.

I have had some parents tell me that they do not believe in disciple with regards to their Star children. Most of the time, it is not necessary for them to tell me. The noise level in the home is an immediate tip off. If these parents are equating discipline with punishment, I agree with them. However, there is a big difference between setting limits and punishment. Children need and cry out for limits.

Robert Gerard, a lecturer, author and father of a Star child, has coined the term "Loving Discipline" which is discipline with the intent of serving the child's "spiritual" interests. He says that these new (Indigo) children demand to be informed of those life experiences that do not serve their highest good"[8].

Children, in fact, want to be children. They do not want the responsibilities of adults. Once, I visited a home outside London where there were three children. The parents were of the belief that they were caretakers for their children's souls, and therefore, their children needed no guidance and always knew perfectly well exactly what they should do. There were no limits for these children, ages twelve to eighteen. This meant they could eat when they wanted, have friends over anytime, play music as loud as they wanted, and so on.

It was interesting to note that the eldest was anorexic and the youngest was always having accidents. I believe these children were shouting out for guidance. They had emptiness about them - a sadness. Could it be that they were interpreting their parents philosophy as not being loving? Were they suffering from *not* being nurtured?

A very dear friend of mine told me this story. Once she was teaching an art class to little children and they were all over the place, shouting, throwing things and generally making a mess. This went on for a few sessions. Then one day, she walked over and calmly picked up a little boy who was the known "trouble maker". She lifted him swiftly straight off the ground. She said his eyes were like saucers. She said, "Enough." After that, the children stopped all their misbehaving and got down to the business of creating and the little boy that she picked up became her good friend.

These were upper middle class little children who, at home, were running wild. They were grateful to have someone set the limits, and then at last they could have real fun. I know this friend's gentle nature well enough to say that she was not controlling the class by using fear tactics. She just cared enough to say, "Stop". Of course, I also know that there are now policies where teachers dare not touch a child, even out of love or sympathy and that is a very sad commentary on my birth country, the U.S.A., and others.

So what kinds of limits should be set on Star children?

Please read this next section with discrimination and those ideas that do not seem appropriate, eliminate them. These ideas are ones that I have formulated over the years from having my own Star child, being a teacher, observing families in their homes, and listening to parents and children. I believe that Star children need guidance perhaps more than the average child because of their strong memories of another way to live. Furthermore, because their mission is to be peacemakers, they really do need the basic tools and skills to function in society. Of course, many Star children will never have to sit down to a formal dinner, as there are as many ways to bring peace as there are colors in the rainbow.

So, please see the following as general guidelines to be regulated by you, the parent, bearing in mind your child's idiosyncrasies. Maybe I am old fashioned, but here they are:

Regular hours and time schedule

All children do best with an adequate amount of rest, but this is really mandatory for Star children. Whenever they get tired, they have a more difficult time coping with everything around them. Their energy is depleted and their "shields" of protection are weak. Most Star children, like most adults, need eight hours of sleep. More and more, I have been hearing of children who need very little sleep – as little as four hours each night. In most households this would be a real problem. So if you happen to have a child like this, they may go into their room at a reasonable hour with some things to amuse themselves like games, books, puzzles, etc. Almost more important than actually sleeping is the time needed to be alone and reconnect with their source, which they should be encouraged to do. (See Chapter Six, Part II)

Believe it or not, most children like routine. They like to know that there is a bedtime, a playtime and meal times. They will flourish with so little guidance. Please, I do not mean that a rigid routine must be followed every day, just that there should be some things, which are more or less at the same time. Children do not need to eat the dinner meal at 6 p.m. sharp, but they do need to know that at sometime around that hour, dinner will be served to them. And if you are in a country where dinner is served at 8 p.m. or 9 p.m., then they need to know that around 5 p.m. they may have small refreshment.

My mother had a very nice after school routine for us. We came home, had a snack, studied and then played before dinner. Of course, there were days where all routine was thrown out the window, for instance, when we went into town or when family members arrived. I will never forget coming home from school and smelling cigar smoke. Oh, yes, I knew my Grandpa Pastroni had arrived and what fun we would have. He loved to disrupt all routine and everything reasonable and logical. How I loved him!

Manners

We need to prepare our Star child to be socially acceptable in order to fulfill his or her peace mission. Until the time that our level of consciousness is such that we no longer judge each other by outward appearances, teaching your children manners is a useful gift you can give them. When a person is polite, optimistic and kind, he or she naturally is in a better position to bring peace to others. So let us look at some of the common pitfalls parents make with their Star children.

One of the most loving things we can teach our children is to listen to others and not interrupt. Just because you may think your child is a Star child and that everything he or she says is important, doesn't mean that others around you will feel the same way. So when you are speaking with another adult your child's input will just have to wait.

You can explain that when you are talking to someone or listening to him or her, you expect your child to be polite and wait until you are through before they speak. This is no different than when you are listening to your child. You would not expect an adult to interrupt either. And, of course, if your child is speaking to another child, you should not interrupt.

Shouting, hitting and throwing things, even in a temper are not allowed because they are unloving things to do. In my opinion, most aggressive behavior occurs when either one of the parents are themselves aggressive towards their child or when the parents give up their authority to their child.

When you first begin to practice some of these suggestions, you may have to remind yourself many times that you are the parent and your child is just that, especially if you have previously allowed your child to have the run of the household.

I have seen children throw food at the dinner table, storm away from the table, throw things at adults, shout at them, hit them and kick them – all with the parents standing passively by, smiling and telling me what a "special" Star child they have. I have heard children scream in restaurants while their parents happily eat. I have actually asked to be moved in restaurants and in planes.

Children are wonderful and they have to learn to function in society, which means parents must guide them. Remember, while Star children have certain unusual gifts, they can be just as stubborn and strong minded as the next.

Once, I was on an airplane with a child kicking the back of my seat. I politely asked the child to stop. The parents looked at me as if I were from outer space (which I am!). The child continued and I finally asked the parents if they could please get their child to stop kicking my seat. They again gave me that look. I pushed the button for the flight attendant, explained the problem, and was moved. These kinds of incidents are completely unnecessary. They can occur only when parents give up their rightful authority.

One of the best ways that I know to set limits, which always worked for me both as a parent and as a teacher, is to practice "time out". This means that if your child is misbehaving, which by the way is for you to decide, you gently take the child and ask him or her to take a few minutes out and to reflect on his or her behavior. You may also tell them that you are not happy when they (fill in the blank: i.e., kick, bite, etc.) and that they need to stay by themselves until they can behave.

You may also need to spell out your expectations. For instance, you might say, "As long as you throw food, you are not welcome at the table. We don't throw food at you and we won't allow you to throw food at us." Then you leave the child alone. Sometimes, this must be repeated many times over, but in the end, you and your child will be happier. When you, as a parent, exercise your authority, you can do so in a calm, firm, and loving manner, which is practically a requirement when dealing with a Star child. Shouting, threats or emotionally charged words do not work, nor does making the child feel guilty.

Of course, it is best if you can be consistent, but as one therapist pointed out, no one is consistent. I believe in setting limits on the big things and letting the small things go. Your aim here is to have a well-adjusted child, not a robot, and surely not a perfect one! Some things like a child's mood, which is so changeable, may be overlooked. So if your child pouts, for example, you may just decide to say and do nothing. Mostly, I believe in setting limits when the child is disrupting the family, friends and guests.

Some children refuse to answer when someone poses a question and are allowed to do so. If your child can talk, then he or she should answer when someone asks a question. Just as we as adults are expected to do so. I have an "adult" friend who won't always answer me when I ask him a question. Do you really want your child to grow up with such an unpleasant, socially unacceptable behavioral trait?

While discussing this subject, I think that most limits are the results of knowing and using common sense politeness. For instance, table manners are learned and are important. You should teach your child simple things such as chewing with our mouths closed, not talking when our mouths are full, which fork to use, and so on.

I once met a New Age type at a retreat center that went on and on about how everyone should eat with his fingers and not use utensils. I thought about handing him a chocolate mousse! How would he be perceived at a peace conference dining with his fellow delegates?

When I moved to France, people were kind enough to show me correct socially acceptable manners. This helped me immensely in being accepted into society, and I am talking here about normal everyday folks, not the upper class. Lessons in politeness could well serve many people both at home and abroad. When someone shows us a kindness, is it too much to say thank you? When we pass someone in the hall, is it possible to smile and say good evening?

Character Building

We can teach our children to be kind, to be polite, and to have a happy demeanor. A simple smile can bring peace to the world. Star children are here to be peacemakers, but they are not here to be treated special or to be made to feel that way. I was very matter of fact with Marcus' gifts and remembrances, as if he were perfectly "normal". It was perhaps a bit easier for me than for a parent who is not also a Star child; however, do teach your child to be polite. It is just so important. Life can be so serious. It is important to have fun, to smile and to laugh. And a child can have tons of fun and still be socially agreeable.

Recently, I attended a conference on peace and religion at UNESCO in Paris. On and on it went, with many people complaining and even some attacking each other. I did not have an experience of peace while I was there. Finally, on my way out, having decided to leave early, a woman in her eighties grabbed my arm. She said she still had hopes for peace because my smile gave her courage to believe in the possibility. I am mentioning this not to say that I have an extraordinary smile, but to give an example of what a sunny person can bring to others in a very simple way. Don't you love to talk to happy people?

A tired, complaining, contrary child will grow up to be a tired, complaining, contrary adult. We must encourage good humor, the capacity to laugh at ourselves, and the courage to continue on in the face of apparent defeat. Star children have an important mission to fulfill. They are born with "extra knowledge", but not necessarily with superior capacities to socialize. We, as parents, teachers and therapists must give them the inner discipline necessary to succeed. And this means, we must teach them to be polite in honoring themselves and others.

Teaching Respect

We must teach our children to respect themselves and others. This means that you as parents must respect others in order to teach your children. It is interesting to me how many parents expect to be respected, yet do not respect their children. A simple gesture like knocking before you enter your child's bedroom can mean a lot. If you respect your child's privacy, he or she will respect yours and won't barge into your bedroom or office unannounced.

When a child respects nature, he won't hurt a tree by carving his initials in it or breaking its branches. He won't kill insects or animals needlessly or maybe not at all. He or she will love the Earth and be grateful for its marvelously intricate systems that support all life here. This understanding will spill over into respect for other people's possessions and for the society in which she or he lives.

Isn't respect a way of showing love for one another and everything around us? We can teach our children that we are all connected. When we hurt someone, we also hurt ourselves because we will feel sad or guilty. Every time we do something kind for another person, we feel pleased and even joyful. Why is this? It is because we are all an expression of the Divine Essence, thus we are all One and there is no real possibility to be separated, one from another.

I read a lovely poem that can guide you in sharing the idea of being connected with your children. The beloved mystical Persian poet, Hafiz, wrote it in the fourteenth century.

IF GOD INVITED YOU TO A PARTY

If God
Invited you to a party
And said,
"Everyone
In the ballroom tonight
Will be my special
Guest,"

How would you then treat them
When you
Arrived?

Indeed, indeed!

And Hafiz knows
There is no one in this world

Who
Is not upon
His Jeweled Dance
Floor.

Limiting Input

Here I like to use the example of a computer. If you fill your computer with garbage, it will produce garbage. We say, "Garbage in, garbage out". And it is the same with our children. Star children are extremely sensitive to negative input. This means we must be careful how we phrase our "limiting" of them. We must also be clear that we are limiting or disapproving of a behavior, not of their essence. We must also be aware of what they are "taking in" as far as what newspapers, magazines and books they read and what television programs and movies they are watching.

Anything violent or frightening can have a very deep impact on them because they are from a place where these things do not exist. I know that I cannot tolerate any type of violence and severely limit my intake of it. I find all aggressive language extremely violent and will move away from anyone who uses it. My friends may think I am hypersensitive, but I am convinced that everyone is affected by everything they experience. It is just that many people do not realize it.

Isn't it better to have a steady diet of positive thoughts and happy events than to live from one catastrophic event to the next as seen in the media? I am not saying that we should bury our heads in the sand, though that is not a bad idea considering media coverage. I am aware of this: where I put my thoughts, my energy goes there and grows. This means that if I constantly look at problems and negative things, that is what I will end up having more of in my life. If I focus on health, abundance, and positive things, I have every possibility of experiencing them. So wouldn't it be a giant step forward to teach our children about positive intentionality? Of course, I know there is not always a direct immediate line between our thoughts and the results, but positive happy thoughts surely contribute to fostering peace in the world.

This morning I received an e-mail that contained a "Memo from God". It said that if we have a problem, which we cannot resolve, we should put it in the box marked, "SFGTD" "Something for God to do". Once we put it there God will solve it in His/Her time and not in our time. Once we put the problem in the box we need to leave it there. Wouldn't it be a nice idea to make a box like that for your child? You could call it the God box, Angel box, or give it whatever label you like. It is a great way to help your child solve a problem without focusing on the problem itself.

Self discipline

We must teach our children to have their own limits as far as their "wants" are concerned. As we move more into the spiritual realms, we will by necessity have less desire for material things. Simple living will become not only acceptable, but in some circles almost obligatory. Normally, Star children are not very interested in material things, so this usually is not a problem.

Through your example, a child naturally learns the difference between needing and wanting, between living simply and conspicuous consumption. It is sad to see people in the more prosperous countries constantly buying and discarding things that are perfectly good.

If you can teach your child to put off instant gratification in return for waiting for something of greater value, you will have taught him or her a valuable lesson. It takes discipline to accomplish a task, to materialize something, or to do just about anything. How would I write this book if I were not disciplined enough to sit at my computer and perhaps forego some other activities which I might imagine to be more fun? It is all a matter of priorities, and helping your child set good priorities is part of your job. And even when a child makes poor choices, she or he is learning, just as we all are every day of our lives.

One way to teach a child values is to discuss possible choices. For instance, if my son wanted to play and not do his homework, I might say something like this, *"It's fine with me if you play and don't do your homework, but you will have to explain in school tomorrow why it's not done."* Or *"I know it might seem to be more fun to play outside than to work. How can you do both? Could you play and run for half an hour and then would you feel like doing your homework?"*

This way you are not making all the decisions for your child. In fact, give your children the information they need to make their own decisions at the earliest age possible. In this way, she or he takes responsibility for his or her actions. Who knows what is more valuable in the long run – to play or to learn math?

Unfortunately, I know too many people who choose to do nothing or to play instead of work and move towards a goal, and if you observe closely, you will see that they achieve very little in life. To be successful, one must have discipline, plain and simple, and here I don't mean success in the generally thought of way. I mean being successful by expressing all that you are and accomplishing all that you came here to do. Everyday, I try to do at least one thing to improve myself, whether it is perfecting French, exercising or reading an uplifting book. We can be examples for our children.

Sense of the Divine

One way to give your child strength to face whatever may lie ahead in life is to teach him about the Divine, whether you perceive that as God, Love, Universal Energy, or whatever term you use. It is good to have a perceptive on life that we are one of the many creatures that exist on Earth and that it is not through our own doing that we can live. In other words, there is "something" which keeps it all going, all together and we need to have a sense of awe when we think of the miracle of our existence. Life is so precious and often times so short, that it is a wonder to be enjoyed. The sense of the Divine can be fostered in many ways, some of which will be discussed in Chapter Seven, Part II.

Our children are expressions of the Divine and so are we. When we come to a state of awareness that whatever happens to one of us in some way happens to all of us and that we are individuals but not separate, real peace will be realized. Planting this seed of understanding in your children will help them to be tolerant of others, their different beliefs, religious or otherwise, and to feel the richness of the diversity of human culture.

"When will we teach our children in school what they are? We should say to them: Do you know what you are? You are a marvel. You are unique. In all of the world there is no other child exactly like you. In the millions of years that have passed there has never been another child like you. And look at your body – what a wonder it is! Your legs, your arms, your cunning fingers, the way you move! . . Yes you are a marvel. And when you grow up, can you then harm another who is, like you a marvel?"[9] Isn't this a revolutionary idea? To actually teach our children how extraordinary they are and how precious all life is?

Chapter Six:

Staying on Track: Interlinking Circles

It seems that many Star children are right on track with understanding their "work" and their collective mission, at least when they are young. Often around the age of twelve, the child, having reached adolescence, is swayed away from his uniqueness and attempts to become more like his peers. And with this immersion into "normalcy" many of the child's psychic gifts are forgotten or lost temporarily. For those that make this passage, there is frequently a catastrophic or a sudden unexpected event that reawakens them to their path later in life.

It is always a judgment call on the part of parents when their child falls into forgetfulness. Sometimes, there is a great relief that the child finally seems to have forgotten all the "strange" things that he once said or did. I cannot give blanket advice to cover every situation, however, if no harm seems to be coming to your child through this forgetful stage, I probably would not do much. However, whenever psychic abilities go "underground" there is a consequence.

If your child develops an eating disorder, starts to drink too much, uses drugs, or shows a complete lack of interest in life, this should be like a red flag going up. Some Star children who have never developed a strong tie to Earth existence may attempt suicide, actively or passively. The will to "go back to their star" can be that strong.

Dr. Orloff believes that ignoring the psychic part of ourselves can "lead to depletion and depression. It is like trying to function on only two cylinders when we have a turbo-charged engine that can travel at lightning speeds. We putter along, make do, but suffer from the chronic drain, our energy reserves wasted"[10].

If we see that a Star child is in trouble then we must seek out competent help. Remember earlier in the book, I suggested that you keep a journal about your Star child's beliefs and unusual happenings and achievements? Well, now is the moment to take out that journal that was kept when the child was younger. Just reminding a Star child of who she really is and why she is here can often provide enough incentive to get back on track.

Star children make deep and profound connections with the Earth and can feel instantly rejuvenated after just a few hours outside in nature. Star children need to connect with the cosmos and react most favorably to physically observing the stars and moon. A camping trip or an excursion into nature may be just what is needed. You may sit quietly and gaze up at the night sky and make some "cosmic comments". Here are some examples, again speak only your truth. You might say something like, *"Gee, when I look at the stars, I know we aren't alone. What do you think or feel?"* or *"Do you remember when you told me you were from another star?"* or *"I remember the time when you told me you were from another star."* (And then relate the experience)

You will be doing your child a great favor by helping her link back to her source. You can also tie in the idea of a peace mission while you are talking. Of course, you must be prepared for any reaction. Your Star child may tell you that you are being silly if she or he is still in denial. She or he may walk away without saying anything. Or, and this is the moment when the stars seem to be shining down just on you and your child, she or he may open up and begin to remember. Thus the road of healing and reintegration of the real self with the created persona begins.

So the interlinking circles are as vast as the universe and as intimate as linking back within your "inner space" to your higher self. We all have an inner knowing or guidance. In our quiet time, we are able to access this part of ourselves. Star children particularly enjoy guided visualizations that have to do with the stars, light, and anything that twinkles or glitters. There is a guided visualization at the end of this chapter that can be very helpful to your child. A good time to use it is during that in between period of wakefulness and sleep.

Because Star children are the problem solvers of tomorrow, they need to be in touch with their creative essence. This is yet another "link" that needs to be kept alive in them. All sorts of artistic and musical expression help them keep in touch with their "world". Seek out creative, positive teachers for your children and stay away from those who offer criticism as a way for your child to "improve" his or her skills.

One perceptive father told me, "We must pay attention not to crush the spirit or light within a child." The interlinking circle back to their home star or to the creative life-giving force of the universe is a precious link and must be respected.

We can also teach our children the "100% Solution". It is very simple. In every situation, just give all you have. And if you do that, you can never lose because you did your best. So you "receive everything", whether you get what you want or not. I use it in my own life and it is very satisfying. No matter what the outcome, I win!

Many Star children love to solve practical problems and they are usually very good at it even at an extremely early age. Give them the opportunity to exercise this skill by asking them how they would handle a household problem. For example, you may have one child who wants to play loud music and another who wants peace and quiet. Ask the children to figure out a solution. Could one listen to music with earphones? Or listen to music while the other is out of the house? Could one child wear earplugs? You see, by doing this you are teaching them to live peacefully together in harmony. This is an important skill to teach because we are all interlinking all the time in all ways with each other.

These interlinking circles include helping Star children connect with other Star children and adults. There are some websites already established for this purpose where there are chat rooms for Star children. However, there is nothing better and more pleasing to your child than meeting another real live Star child or adult right here on Earth. There are more and more organizations for these children, which can be easily found. I have listed some under "Resources" in the back of the book. Again, do a bit of research into the ideas and beliefs of these organizations before you suggest them to your children. Some of the beliefs put forth can be pretty amazing, but who am I to say they aren't true?

There is nothing more beautiful than seeing Star children together. The light around them is lovely and they seem to be able to talk in short hand, using a language all of their own. I suspect that much information is being exchanged with the eyes and on other levels than speaking. At the *Festival for New Children* in Holland, many children sought me out because they had read the book, which I have written, entitled *Star Child*. They wanted to see Marcus' mother and they asked a lot of questions about him. Since he is not on the Earth plane anymore, they were very interested in knowing where he was and if I could still talk to him. I explained the mystery of it all as best as I could.

The festival took place in a forest and what a delightful sight it was to see two young girls with their arms around each other's neck. They approached me rather shyly to tell me that they had discovered that they were from the very same star. The excitement of it all! And I was sure that they would be friends for life. Many of the children made instant connections with children of the same vibration and were happily sharing all the things that they couldn't share with other children.

Once at the festival, I was outdoors with a large number of children who were engaged in making hand held rattles out of paper maché. The man who was teaching them has a lovely soul; he also happens to be almost blind. It was such a blessing to watch him work with these Star children. It was truly love in action.

At one point, I took a rattle and sat on the ground looking for small pebbles to put in it. Suddenly, a little girl of about two years was standing silently in front of me. I handed her the rattle. She carefully selected stone after stone to put into the rattle, listening each time to the new sound it made. Each time she added a stone, she attentively listened to the new sound, then she shook her head "no" and continued working. This went on for quite a few minutes before finally, she smiled. The sound of the rattle had her approval. She handed it back to me and dashed away. Hours later when it was finished, she was there again. Of course, I handed her the rattle. She smiled and ran away. Now there is an example of creativity and ancient memory working hand in hand!

Also, it was great to see the parents sitting together and talking at the festival. They, however, seemed to be having a more difficult time "with all of this". I believe many of them were surprised and delighted to find that their child wasn't alone or unique. On the other hand, I felt that parents need support too and that these interlinking circles can extend to them as well.

Support groups are so helpful if people can come together, share their experiences, and leave with a feeling of encouragement and hope.

Unfortunately, it is my experience that many support groups tend to dwell on the negative, on problems. So if you decide to join one, be sure that the person facilitating the group has a positive attitude. The quickest way to ascertain the perspective of the group facilitator is to share something positive that has happened in your life. If little attention is given to a positive sharing and most of the attention goes to those with problems, well, you have your answer, don't you?

We must also trust the overall process. Your Star child will find his or her way. She or he will connect with other Star children or adults when it is the right time. However, you should be alert to all possible openings and opportunities to aid your child in making those connections. We are all connected, all part of the Universal Divine Plan which is far greater and more mysterious than most of us will ever know, at least while we are here in our bodies.

Interlinking Circles – A Guided Visualization

For those of you, who are not familiar with this technique, a guided visualization is a method often used in relaxation therapy. One person reads or speaks out loud words that have a specific goal in mind, for instance, relaxation. The following visualization, which is written in two versions, one for younger children and the other for older children, has as its goal to help your child remember she or he is connected to everyone and everything and that there is plenty of love and support in the universe.

Please feel free to change the wording as you see fit. I believe short visualizations are just as effective as long ones. Personally, I get tired of too many words and too much guidance, so I leave a lot to the imagination of the child who is listening. When a guided visualization is too tightly planned and too directive, your child may experience a sense of failure if she or he is not able to visual what you are saying.

Whenever I use visualization, I always tell participants to follow whatever they are experiencing and to not be concerned if their experience doesn't correspond to what I am saying. It often happens that children go off to a completely different "place" and that's very fine too. Before the visualization, I include some introductory material appropriate for each age level. Remember to read slowly with plenty of pauses. Of course, if your child has certain fears, you must alter the visualization to accommodate them.

Visualization for a Star child approximately six to twelve years old

This is a bedtime meditation. Please remember to turn off your phones and to tell other family members not to disturb you during this time.

"Mommy (or Daddy) is (or I am) going to read something to you and you can imagine the story taking place, just like you do when you're dreaming. If I say something and you imagine something else, that's all right. Whatever you see or feel is just fine. There's no right or wrong way. This should be a fun time – let's see what happens when we do this together.

Okay, now, are you comfy? And ready to begin? Do you need anything before we start (like a glass of water, etc.)? No, okay, so just lie down and get all snuggly (like a little bear), close your eyes, and listen to Mommy's (or Daddy's) (or my) voice. Sometimes, I might ask you a question, but you don't have to answer me, just listen.

Imagine that you are sitting on a big pillow way up in the sky and that it's a bright sunny day. This pillow isn't just any ordinary pillow, it's a pillow filled with magic and it can take you anywhere in the whole universe. Can you see your pillow? I hope that it is a pretty color that you like, maybe even your favorite color. You can make the pillow any color you want. The pillow is nice and soft and big enough for all of you to fit on it. So there you are just floating along feeling the sun shining down on you.

Now you decide that it would be fun to go far, far away to another star or planet and off you zoom through space. It's funny, but the minute you think about going, your pillow takes you there. It's magic after all. So now, you've landed on this star so far away. Look around you. What do you see? How do you feel? Is it cold or warm there? Do you smell anything special? Do you hear anything, see anyone? This star is very beautiful, and there are only friendly things there. Maybe you'll see giant flowers, or fountains with root beer in them, or someone old and wise like Grandpa or Grandma who might want to tell you a secret. If you do see someone like that, go ahead and listen to what they have to tell you. Shhh. Let's listen quietly.

Just imagine all sorts of wonderful things. This is your magical star, your magical time, and anything can happen here. So take a few minutes and enjoy yourself. I'm just going to be quiet while you are having fun. (Pause and watch your child's eye movements and facial expression. This should be every enjoyable.)

Now, we are going to go back to your magic pillow and imagine that you zoom back and fly around the Earth. Look at all the beautiful things on Earth, the trees, the animals, the oceans, and all the different people working, playing, eating, and studying. Isn't it fun to see the Earth from up above? Finally, you decide to land and down you go right into your bed and into your body. Feel yourself here in your body. Do you feel the bed covers around you? What do you hear besides my voice? (Pause)

Now, imagine that your magic pillow is teeny and you are safely on it and you can fly into your heart. Go there and feel all the love that everyone has for you. Feel all the love of the angels, of your pets, of the trees and flowers, and of God. (Change the language here to fit your belief system)

Think about everything that went right for you today. All the times you were happy and having fun. (Pause) *All the happy times you've ever had in your whole life are stored in your heart and anytime you are sad, you can go on your magic pillow right into your heart and remember those times.* (Pause) *Now make yourself big like you really are and feel yourself back here with Mommy (or Daddy) (or in the room). After all that traveling you should be tired and ready to sleep. If you want you can just fall to sleep or you can open your eyes now and let's have a big hug.*

(If your child isn't already asleep, ask him or her to share the experiences she or he had. And then say good night with hugs and kisses.)

Guided Visualization for the older child and for adult Star children

This is a bedtime meditation. Be sure to turn off your phones so you won't be disturbed and tell other members of the family not to disturb you.

Let's try this guided visualization together. Are you ready to begin? I'm going to read the visualization to you and you can go on an imaginary journey by listening to the words. If I say something and you imagine something else, that's all right. Whatever you see or feel is just fine. There's no right or wrong way. Let's just have fun and see what happens when we do this together.

Get into a comfortable position and try to let go and leave behind you all the things that happened today and relax. Okay, now close your eyes, and just listen to my voice. You might want to imagine yourself getting heavier and feeling more peaceful while lying on your bed, warm and safe. Sometimes, I might ask you a question, but you don't have to answer me, you can just listen. This is your time to explore and go on a relaxing journey.

Imagine that you are lying on the ground in a soft comfortable sleeping bag out in nature in one of your most favorite places. You might be in the mountains at a camping site, on the sand by the ocean, in a clearing by a rushing river, or anywhere else that you like. (Pause) *It's a clear night and you can feel a slight breeze passing across your face, and you are at peace. You are amazed when you look up into the night sky. You are out in full nature very far from city lights and perhaps that's why the stars seem especially bright. In fact as you look up, you see one special star that seems to glow brighter than all the others do. Could that be your special star? The star where you're from?*

As the star grows brighter and brighter, you find yourself feeling drowsy, there under the stars, and your eyes begin to gently close. As you close your eyes, you find yourself drifting back in time to another place and another space. To a time and space in a different realm, on another star that you remember so well. You continue to drift further and further away until you find yourself actually standing on your star. Now I don't know where you are exactly, that's for you to know. While you are rather surprised to be there, you feel at home, happy to see all the things that are so familiar to you. Take a few minutes to look around. What do you see? Do you have friends there? What do you feel? Are there familiar odors or sounds? Just take your time. (Pause)

Now imagine that you notice, out of the corner of your eye, that there is someone standing near you. When you see this being, you have the feeling in your heart that you are meeting an old friend. And you feel calm and happy about it. Now I don't know who that being is or what he or she looks like, maybe it's someone old, or someone you've known before, or someone very wise. That's for you to decide. As the being comes closer, he or she begins to talk to you. There's an important message for you, perhaps an answer to a question or a solution to a problem that has been bothering you. You listen. (Pause)

When you feel like it, you thank the wise being for his or her guidance. And, when you feel ready, you begin to leave your star that you love so much, knowing that you can go there again and again in your imagination or in your dreams; but that for right now, you need to come back to Earth and fulfill your mission here. So slowly, so slowly and gently, you begin to come back into your body, which is still lying under the stars out in your favorite setting in nature. You hear the familiar sounds of Earth – maybe the ocean waves or the rushing river and you feel peaceful. (Pause)

Whatever information you were given by the wise being that you met, you safely guard in your heart. And as you put that little gift of guidance and love in your heart, you suddenly feel grateful to be alive in your body which functions so well here on Earth. You begin to remember all the good things that you have in your life and you are thankful for them. (Pause)

And now, you begin to see within your heart a little shining star, the radiant person that you really are. And that little star begins to grow and get brighter as you remember more clearly why you came to Earth and what you must do to fulfill your life mission. And you are happy and peaceful, with a soft smile on your face. (Pause)

And now, you find yourself leaving that place in nature that you had so carefully selected. You find yourself coming back into your own bed, or into the room where we are together. You gradually become aware of the sounds and odors around you as you start to come back fully into your body, remembering everything that happened to you on your journey. You feel the weight of the cover and the softness of the bed beneath your body. You have crystal clear memories of everything that you experienced and everything that was told to you. You remember all the information that you received and can use it right here on Earth. Now gradually, you begin to move around and finally you open your eyes. (If your child is sleeping at this point, you may eliminate the last sentence and just leave the room, if you choose.)

If your child opens his eyes, you may ask him if he wishes to share anything about the experience with you, or if not, perhaps he would like to write down a few notes or draw something in order not to forget the information received.

And no matter what the age of your child, it is always nice to have a hug before going to sleep, wish each other sweet dreams, and pray together if you like.

These visualizations will help your child have positive thoughts and a sense of his or her real power. One of the things that we can teach our children is how to "stay on track" with who they really are. We can do this by teaching them about controlling their thoughts. "Thought is more powerful than an automatic rocket. In less than one second, you can go wherever you want, experience closeness to anyone, or adopt whatever state of mind you wish"[11]. We can all learn to say, "No, stop!" to negative thoughts and turn our minds to loving, helpful thoughts. When we teach our children to dwell on worthwhile thoughts, we are giving them a storehouse of riches for future use. Why not teach our children to have beautiful thoughts (after we teach ourselves, of course)?

John Ruskin, noted English author, gives us some ideas: "To get peace if you want it, make for yourselves nests of pleasant thoughts. None of us yet know, for none of us have been taught in early youth, what fairy palaces we may build of beautiful thoughts – proofs against all adversity: bright fancies, satisfied memories, noble histories, faithful sayings; treasure-houses of precious and restful thoughts which care cannot disturb, nor pain make gloomy, nor poverty take away from us – houses built without hands, for our souls to live in."

Chapter Seven:

Creating Magical Spaces

Magical spaces can be created anywhere, right in your own home, in your garden and even in your child's school. Star children especially like ritual and sacred spaces, mainly because they are super sensitive to energy. There are many, many good books about creating these spaces, however, I would like to tell you about some that I have created and used that have worked very well.

Making an Altar

One idea which children love is to make an altar. Now before you immediately decide that an altar is "too religious", please give the idea a chance by reading further on. An altar can serve a variety of purposes. First and foremost, it gives your home a spiritual focus. Altars or sacred spaces in living spaces are traditionally used in many cultures and are considered perfectly normal. In most western cultures, it is probably best if you choose a space in your home where your guests rarely go and certainly one where you will not be easily disturbed. I traditionally have altars in my bedroom for example and once even made one on top of a safe in the biggest closet I ever had!

In addition to providing a focus on the spiritual aspect of life, an altar provides a place where dreams, wishes, problems, and difficult circumstances may be handed over to Angels, God, or another higher power. It's a focal point where you and your children can sit quietly and reflect on your day, and where you can regain your courage and strength. To me, an altar in the home is more necessary than a table to eat on because without inner strength our meals give us little nourishment.

The simplest way to make an altar is on a small table or other piece of furniture. It needs to be at a height that your child can see, so not up too high. Since it is a place to honor the sacred, it should be a clean, light space. You may choose to cover the table with a lovely cloth. I have found that light, soft colors are more relaxing than loud colors, but this is a personal preference. Some people believe that the altar must face the east, which in some traditions represents the birthplace of spiritual power. Others believe that it must face another direction. My belief is that one direction is not necessarily better than another, since spirit is everywhere, so just place it where you like. Of course, should you have a specific belief, then do look up what is best in your tradition.

Once you have decided on the place for your altar and you have set up and covered the table, you and your children are ready to "furnish" it with objects that are meaningful. Most of what you will use, you already have on hand. I don't believe in running out and buying all sorts of things. The most powerful altars are homemade! Again, for me there is nothing, which absolutely has to be on your altar. Having said this, I will tell you the objects that are always on mine. I love candles and often have them burning in my home to remind me of the light of spirit. If you have very small children, of course, you must place a candle in an enclosure in order to create the least danger of burns or fire. And you must explain to your children that the candle is special and can only be lit at certain times. I also know people with small children who place electrically lit candles on their altar. A nice supply of fragrant incense and a safe burner adds to the atmosphere. Flowers and small plants are nice additions, bringing in the beauty of nature. Of course, it is very important to include your child in all these selections.

This leads to the idea of sacred objects. I would say that whatever the child wants to place on the altar is fine – free range of choice can be given here. Found objects are often meaningful to children, such as the shells picked up from last summer's vacation or stones, dried flowers and pieces of tree bark gathered on a walk in the woods.

Crystals, little sacred objects and "jewels" bought in shops also belong on the altar. Crystals have been used since ancient times as tools for spiritual, mental and physical healing. I have a very large one on my altar and I am convinced that it is doing a lot of work transforming energy in my home.

Finally, there should be a little container where dreams, wishes, problems and difficult circumstances may be written down and turned over to the Angels. Remember the idea of the "God or Angel" box. This container may be a small box, basket, dish or anything else you have easily available, maybe even something that your child has made.

On my altar I have a rather large angel statue that is holding a basket. There, in that basket, my clients and friends may leave their wishes and troubles behind them. A pencil and a little pad of paper can be kept nearby to write these things down.

There are so many possibilities of objects that the choices are unlimited. You may want to make your altar around a certain theme, such as the holidays of the year or featuring a particular culture. You may have a child who loves Native American teachings for example. Then you can build a medicine wheel on your altar. If your child loves angels, then that could be a theme. I have two angel statues on mine, along with two sets of angel cards. Well, you are limited only by your creative abilities!

Children do love decks of cards. I have a number of them, some in English and since I am living in Paris, some in French. One deck of angel cards has French words on them with cute little pictures. I also have a lovely deck of angel cards with large beautiful pictures and a single word on them in English. There are "medicine" cards with animals and a book that explains the power and wisdom of each animal, based on Native American teachings. Again, the variety is endless and one trip into a metaphysic bookstore will satisfy all your interests and needs.

Some of the books, which go along with the cards, are too difficult for your children to understand; but you can paraphrase the explanations. Children love to pose a question and draw a card. I even have young people who phone me and tell me they are nervous right before an exam. Would I draw a card and tell them what guidance it provides? Often, I give these cards away to people who carry them around in their wallets and purses, sometimes for years.

Altars can be used as a place to recharge your batteries just by sitting in front of them for a few minutes and quietly looking at their beauty. Through them you can reconnect with spirit and help your child to do so too. For instance, let us say your child has had a difficult moment at school. When she or he comes home, you may both sit for a few minutes in front of the altar and then she or he may write down her or his feelings and place it with the angels. You may burn incense or light a candle to transform the energy of the experience. Of course, it is also good to talk about what happened before you place it on the altar for the higher power to deal with it.

One little eight-year-old girl that I know made little altars on shelves in a small bookcase. She had developed rituals that went along with each altar, as each one served a different purpose. I was invited to place a wish in a little shell, which was then placed between some rocks. The whole "ceremony" was imbedded in ritual. When I asked her how she "knew" what to do, she responded that she "just knew." One of the amazing things is that once the altar is constructed, your Star child will "know" what to do and how to use it.

Altars can serve as a focal point for family prayers, celebrations, and rituals. You can give thanks for something good that has happened by placing a small gift like a flower on it. Sitting quietly in front of it, getting away from the business and pressure of life, is very nurturing and can be inspiring. If your child is stuck and does not know how to do something, for instance, a few quiet moments may provide the answer or at least the courage to continue.

How to Meditate and Pray Together

There are many good books out about how to meditate with your child. These are worth exploring. I very much enjoy the books by Thich Nhat Hanh who is a well-known Buddhist monk. He teaches mindfulness in a very simple way and also how to do walking meditation, which is nice for children who have trouble being still. Since there are many different ways to meditate, you will have to find the one that works best for you and your child. One of the easiest ways for a child to meditate is having them observe the breath as I already mentioned.

Here is a simple meditation from Thich Nhat Hanh: "Breathing in, I calm my body." He says, "Reciting this line is like drinking a glass of cool lemonade on a hot day – you can feel the coolness permeate your body. When I breathe in and recite this line, I actually feel my breath calming my body and mind." And then, "Breathing out, I smile." Here he points out, "You know a smile can relax hundreds of muscles in your face. Wearing a smile on your face is a sign that you are master of yourself"[12]. Something as simple as this can change your child's mood in minutes.

Another meditation, which Thich Nhat Hanh tells about in his book, teaches how we can see everything in the universe in a piece of fruit. This is a very practical exercise and can be used, obviously, with any type of fruit. He tells us of this lovely experience: "One day, I offered a number of children a basket filled with tangerines. The basket was passed around, and each child took one tangerine and put it in his or her palm. We each looked at our tangerine, and the children were invited to meditate on its origins. They saw not only their tangerine, but also its mother, the tangerine tree. With some guidance, they began to visualize the blossoms in the sunshine and in the rain. Then they saw petals falling down and the tiny green fruit appear. The sunshine and the rain continued, and the tiny tangerine grew. Now someone has picked it, and the tangerine is here.

After seeing this, each child was invited to peel the tangerine slowly, noticing the mist and the fragrance of the tangerine, and then bring it up to his or her mouth and have a mindful bite, in full awareness of the texture and taste of the fruit and the juice coming out. We ate slowly like that. "Each time you look at a tangerine, you can see deeply into it. You can see everything in the universe in one tangerine. When you peel it and smell it, it's wonderful. You can take your time eating a tangerine and be very happy"[13].

Here is one more idea: Some children like to keep their eyes open and focus on an object, such as a burning candle. You can direct them to just keep looking at it and observing everything about it – its color, how the flame gets larger and smaller, brighter, etc. This causes them to become deeply absorbed in something outside of themselves and helps to reduce tension in difficult situations. It is a very relaxing exercise.

Traditional prayers and ones your children make up can also be repeated in front of your altar. Remember, you must be true to your beliefs and those of your child. If meditation is too "New Age" for you or if you suspect that it may be part of a sect, do not use it. Whatever you do, you must believe in it and so must your child. I was brought up in a church until I was six years old, when I decided that certain beliefs were incompatible with mine. I kept my mouth shut and went through the rituals for the sake of my family, but my belief went out the door at an early age. However, I very much believe in the power of prayer and have seen it work miracles.

When I pray for a certain result, I am wise enough now to add, "this or something better comes to pass" or "under Divine governance" or "if this is best for everyone concerned". It is a good idea to teach your child to pray in this way as well because while we can "control" a lot in our lives, I do not believe I am totally in charge of all the outcomes of my prayers.

Sometimes, a prayer goes apparently unanswered only because it is not for the highest good. It is important to explain this to children. I remember praying that my little brother, Jimmy, would not die, and when he did, I was very angry at God. What had happened to my wishes? My prayer? A very good therapist once reminded me that there is only one God and that while I may have a Divine soul, I am not running the show!

Emmet Fox, a spiritual teacher who has a commonsense approach, shares his ideas about unanswered prayers. He says, "Strangely enough, it often happens that we receive an answer to our prayer and do not recognize it." He then gives a great example that can be used with a child. "If a boy prayed for a man's hat (because he thought it would look well on him or make him grown up) he would not get it because Divine Wisdom knows that he could not wear it. He would get a good hat of the sort that would be useful to him. We often pray for things for which we are not really prepared, but if we pray scientifically this will not matter, since Creative Intelligence will send us the thing that we really need. The practice of the Presence of God is the perfect prayer because it understands everything and overlooks nothing"[14].

I have known of parents who meditate, go to support groups and prayer groups, teach spiritual principles to adults, read and even write uplifting books, only to leave their children out of the process completely. It is as if they have an adult spiritual world and then the world with their children. This I find most strange. Perhaps some of these ideas will help those of you in this position to bridge your spiritual beliefs and practices into the world of your children where *it is so desperately needed by them.*

In using your altar, praying and/or meditating with your child, you may want to include sound. There are numerous beautiful meditative CDs to choose from, as well as uplifting songs with inspiring lyrics. Bells, little flutes known as recorders, Tibetan bowls, and hand drums can all add a musical quality to your experience. You may also want to try vocal meditation and prayer by chanting certain phrases over and over again, singing little songs or humming in front of the altar.

Rituals and Activities, Which Acknowledge the Sacred

In addition to prayer, meditation, making altars, you may want to include rituals in your child's life. I know of one mother who starts the day by listening carefully to her children's dreams at the breakfast table. The children like the attention and it helps them to integrate the messages received in their dreams into everyday life. You might want to have a talking stick, from the Native American tradition, or a little stuffed heart on the table. The child who is holding the stick or heart has the right to share. Everyone else must listen. It is important to know that when you are holding the talking object in your hands, no one will interrupt and you are safe to share without interruption. Of course, they must also be on time for school, so for example, you may be the timekeeper and give the child holding the object five minutes to talk.

Another tool, which can help you and your child be positive co-creators in life, is the use of affirmations. An affirmation is a positive statement, which you make in the present tense. You can repeat it silently or out loud, chant or sing it, or just read it. My "bible" for affirmations and positive thinking is the book entitled *The Writings of Florence Scovel Shinn*.[15] While some of her language is a bit outdated and she focuses on Christian terminology, her ideas are current even though she wrote from 1925 to 1945. She points out that when you make up an affirmation it must "click" in order for it to make an impression on the subconscious mind. You can easily transform the affirmations she gives into ones suitable for children.

Some examples that are great for children are: *"I am happy, peaceful, and joyful." "I'm growing stronger and stronger, everyday." "All doors open for me now." "I am successful." "I let go and flow like a river." "I believe in myself."* You can also sing or chant one word over and over, such as "joy", "love", "happy", "smiles", and so on. You can encourage your child to put up signs with affirmations written on them in his bedroom, in the bathroom, anywhere the child goes in the house and you can do the same for yourself. Children often make colorful signs to display. Most children love to do this and it is great for building a positive self-image.

Another ritual consists of burning a smudge stick, which is made up of sage and pine. In the Native American tradition, sage is a purifying and cleansing agent. It can be used to cleanse your child's room, especially if she or he is reporting "bad vibes" in it. The older child enjoys doing this whenever she or he deems it necessary. Be sure to hold a plate under the smudge stick to keep the ashes and sparks from burning holes in things.

You can also clean your child's energy field by passing the smudge stick around his or her body. Remember to hold a plate under the stick. This is very good to use for Star children who "pick up" other people's energy. It puts them right back into their own energy vibration. You might want to add some words, such as, *"Cleansing, cleansing. All energy is becoming light energy."* or *"Out, out – all dirty critters leave right now."* or *"As this smoke rises in the air, it takes with it all negativity and replaces it with good energy."* Well, you get the idea.

One family joins hands at the dinner table every night and says a short prayer and blessing over the food before eating. Another lights a candle and tells the child that the light will protect him throughout the night. Another family, in creating sacred experiences, makes a circle of stones and sits together in it as a symbol of staying together and being present for each other. There, they may pray together, meditate or quietly share ideas and thoughts. A stone circle experience is very good to use when your child has a friend whose parents are getting a divorce. Children often feel threatened by what happens in their friends' families.

If your child is troubled or has to make a decision, you may help her make a circle or triangle of stones in the mountains or on the beach. Tell your child that he can pose a question and go inside the sacred space and wait for the answer that will surely come. A special place in the garden, a bench, a fountain, or even sitting under a certain tree may provide a good substitute for a stone circle. And of course, rituals around death are important. There are many good books about rituals and some are especially written for children.

Some families have "family time", where once a week on a certain evening or afternoon, everyone eats together and afterwards participates in group activities. Every family member agrees to keep that time as sacred for the family. You may have a family meeting, giving everyone an opportunity to "check-in" and tell about his or her week. This is another opportunity to use your talking stick when sharing. Concerns and problems that affect the family can also be raised with solutions and choices forthcoming. You may decide to play games, make puzzles, share music, create something artistic, or engage in any number of activities. You may also read books and stories that encourage discussion. Children of all ages love books like *The Little Prince* and the Harry Potter stories.

The goal is to get to know each other better, to interact and support one another, and to share in a common activity. This "family time" can strengthen every member of the family and will provide sweet memories as well.

The following activities can also be easily integrated into "family time"

Dr. Mansukh Patel and Rita Goswami have written an outstanding book that may help you and your child master your emotions and have better relationships with others. Dr. Mansukh Patel, through the power of walking, has carried out many projects that bring hope and inspiration to people worldwide. The wonderful thing about the book is its exercises of hand and body movements. These exercises help your child integrate positive thoughts and energy into his or her body.

For example, if your child is fearful, maybe she or he can try the "Gesture of Courage" which draws out the courageous lion within us. I especially like this simple exercise since I identify with the lion. "Raise your open hands shoulder height, palms facing forward. (This is the same hand motion that we use to signify stop if we don't want something or if someone is encroaching on our personal space, only here it is done with both hands. It is also the signal a policeman will use to stop traffic.) Draw your hands back towards your chest and feel the shoulder blades squeezed together. Hold for at least ninety seconds"[16].

Here is another example, which is particularly good for Star children who tend to want to live in the stars and not on Earth. "Heart Hug" – Imagine you are holding a tree, your arms hugging the tree at shoulder height. Visualize the strength and power of the tree flowing into you with each in breath and filling your whole body on the out breath. Become a tree, strong and powerful. Affirm: *"I am strong and powerful"*[17]. I think this exercise could be even more powerful if you take your child outside to hug a real tree. If your child feels light headed or detached from the Earth, this is also an excellent exercise to use.

As to being powerful, we are all co-creators with the Divine Force and thus we are unlimited beings. Most of us, however, spend our lives "being small", not daring to be the "masters" that we are. I want to end this book with an idea that is throughout the Kryon information channeled by Lee Carroll, a former businessman in California.

Kryon, a pure love entity, has been invited several times to present his messages through channeling to the United Nations in New York. The information is practical and helpful in our every day lives and for this reason, I have chosen to present it here. In other words, I have saved the most powerful visualization for the last. I have rewritten it in language and concepts appropriate for children, but the idea comes directly from the Kryon material.

The Golden Chair

This is a visualization that can be used anytime, anywhere. Just have your child get relaxed and comfortable and slowly read it out loud to him or her.

Imagine that up in the sky somewhere, maybe even on another star, there is a magical golden room and that you can go there anytime that you wish. This is a special room just for you. Each person has his own room filled with golden light and love. As you enter the room, you feel so much love – it's as if an Angel lives there.

You see a very big chair that is made of real gold. Someone is sitting in the chair – it must be an Angel. But as you dare to come closer, you can barely see the Angel. There's so much light, as if there's a sun inside the room. You slowly walk closer and closer to the chair where the Angel is sitting and you see that the Angel has your face. How can that be, you ask? You move closer and then you realize that the Angel in the chair is who you really are. You are an Angel!

Imagine that you can go and sit on the chair. When you do, you feel that you are like a king or queen or an angel. You have a sparkling crown on your head. It's magical because it connects you to God (or other Angels). And when you wear this crown, you feel so much love for everyone and everything. This is who you really are. You are an Angel, filled with light, love and power.

You can do anything. You have everything you need to be the great person that you are right here on Earth. And anytime you are not sure what to do or when you want to know the answer to something, you can go to your golden room and ask the Angel that you are for help. Your "bigger self" is always there on the other side just waiting to help you. You are big and strong. You can make good things happen because you are part of God.

Whenever you feel small and helpless, remember who you really are! Remember that you can go to your golden room anytime and anywhere. You are always there in the golden chair, with a golden crown on your head, which helps you know why you are here on Earth and how to live your life with love. You are an Angel. [18] (End of visualization).

The image of being an angel in a golden chair can be a very powerful one. It can help your Star child stay connected with the sacred, all-powerful part of him or herself. And it works wonders for those of us who need to reconnect with our God power. You and your child may also decide to cover a chair with a piece of golden cloth and create a real "golden chair". So then whenever your Star child is feeling sad, weak or unclear, she or he can actually sit in the chair of real power, of love, and make a connection with the Divine.

While this may sound like "useless" play, I encourage you to play with your Star child and with each other. Plato says, *"You can discover more about a person in an hour of play than in a year of conversation."* I believe that is true. Life should be a joyous adventure filled with love and laughter. It is in playfulness that our imaginations blossom, that we are drawn more closely to our God source, that we can discover who we truly are.

I have spent many wonderful hours playing with Star children everywhere. Whenever I feel like I'm losing touch with my Angel Self, with my playful essence, I think back on moments of joyful play with some of the Star children that I know: laughing with Julia when she told me her dreams in three languages; boating with Christophe; playing complicated games with Timothé (age 3); dancing with the ultimate Spice Girl, Tamarinde; looking into Rebecca's eyes; laughing with Sam; listening to Mara's stories; painting with AnnaKim; watching Stephan jump out from hiding under the table and the list goes on and on. Thank you, Star children everywhere, for reminding me of who I am. So grab that Star child of yours and start dancing, singing and laughing. The world is a beautiful place. Enjoy it!